Revelation

By

A.J. Messenger

First Print Edition August 2016

ISBN-13: 978-1537241449

ISBN-10: 1537241443

Cover images credit:

Sirikornt | istockphoto.com

Books by A.J. Messenger

The Guardian Series
(a paranormal angel romance series)

Guardian (book one)

Fallen (book two)

Revelation (book three)

More titles from A.J. Messenger coming soon

Learn more about new releases and contact me

I welcome you to visit me at the sites below and subscribe to my newsletter to be the first to know about upcoming releases.

ajmessenger.com

facebook.com/ajmessengerauthor

@aj_messenger

Dedication

To my greatest helper. You know who you are.

Table of Contents

"Question Everything. Find your own light."

– Anonymous

"True love stories never have endings."

– Richard Bach

Preface

In my dream, if it is a dream, the baby is smiling, with wondrous emerald green eyes and a distinct sparkle.

Finn, Liz, and Chief Stephens are all gathered around as my mom holds the baby in her arms with a depth of love I can feel in my heart.

But why is my mom crying? And why does everyone look so sad?

And where is Alexander?

Chapter One

This can't be.

I'm *pregnant?*

I stare at the plus sign on the test in my hand but I still don't quite believe it. Even if it is the seventh test stick I peed on.

It's been six weeks since Alexander took me on our amazing night flight around the world and we made love in our perfect spot in the San Mar Mountains. At first I dismissed the message I remembered from my dad as either a dream or a product of synapses firing in a supremely relaxed state. I mean, *c'mon,* I just made love with an angel, who knows what that can do to a person?

But now, staring at the pregnancy test in my hand, which I purchased on a lark because of a missed period not thinking in a million *years* it would come back positive, I can't help but wonder if my memory of my father's message was real. Alexander said that discovering the truth of what happened could have freed his soul to move on. Maybe he's trying to communicate. And help me. When I think about it, it had to have been my dad who saved me out in the ocean. Otherwise, I honestly can't explain how I made it to shore. And now he's trying to warn me: *Protect the baby. At all costs.*

The baby. Can it really be true that I have a life growing inside me? I place my palm over my stomach and imagine the warm, white light in my core protecting all that's within.

As the shock slowly wears off I smile and imagine the amazingly cute baby Alexander and I would make, but then the reality of the situation breaks through again. I just turned nineteen and I also just started my first year of college two weeks ago. Depending on when exactly this supposedly impossible pregnancy occurred … that would make the baby born before I even complete my first year at UCSM. How is that even going to work? *Sorry professor, I'll have to reschedule my finals because I'll be busy having a baby that day.* I chuckle at my ridiculously pragmatic thoughts and then I whipsaw over to a decidedly panicky feeling in my chest.

But the idea of a baby—*Alexander's* baby—although unexpected, sends such joy through me that I can hardly sit still. I'm meeting him at the beach in an hour to go surfing. I want to tell him but I have no idea how he'll react. He insisted it was impossible for guardians to have babies—they can't extend the line in that way. *Guess angels don't always know everything.*

But what if he's not happy with the news? Or what if this breaks some crazy guardian rule I don't know about? *But how could it break a rule, Declan, if it was supposedly impossible?*

I dismiss all of my meandering worries almost the moment I have them. Alexander has shown me time and again that we talk things through and we're honest with each other. Whatever this means, we'll figure it out together … and he'll be thrilled.

I hope.

Chapter Two

"Do you ever wonder," I ask Alexander as we're walking with our surfboards, "why we were drawn together like we were?" We're nearly down all the steps to the beach.

He looks over at me and smiles. "In one of my lives, my parents were very different but they had an especially good connection. I remember when people used to ask my mum how they managed to get on so well she used to smile and say: '*There's no greater mystery than whom we spark to and why.*' I never realized how true that was until I sparked to you."

"You think we're very different?" I ask.

"No," he laughs, "we're actually a lot alike. I've just never sparked to someone the way I sparked to you."

I smile. I like that term *sparked*. It perfectly encapsulates how I felt when I saw Alexander for the first time. And every time I see him, in fact. "Do you think," I ask, "that if two people like us spark together, that something impossible can happen?"

We reach a good spot on the beach and he sets down his backpack and jabs his surfboard into the sand and looks over at me. "Sure," he says, "anything is possible … but I don't understand, where is this going?"

"If anything is possible," I say as he's pulling up his wetsuit and maneuvering his arms in, "is it possible I could be pregnant?"

He yanks the long pull tab to zip up the back of his wetsuit and looks at me. "*What?*"

"We've had sex," I say. "A lot."

He smiles wryly. "Yes, if two mortals had sex as often as we have without protection, pregnancy would definitely be on the table. But I'm a guardian, we can't have progeny, it doesn't work that way."

"But what if I *am* pregnant?"

He stares at me for a long beat. "What are you saying?"

I swallow. "I'm saying that I bought seven different pregnancy tests from the drugstore and they all came up positive."

He grabs onto the surfboard in the sand beside him. "Are you serious?"

I smile. "Yes."

"How can that be?" I detect a flash of what looks like fear in his eyes, alarming me. But just as quickly a range of other emotions play over his face until eventually he settles on a very slow, very astounded smile. He walks toward me with surprised, joyful eyes and lifts me into his arms, spinning us around. "You're *pregnant?*"

I nod and he brings me back down so he can plant an exuberant kiss on my lips.

"How?" he asks.

"The usual way, I guess."

He laughs. "This isn't supposed to be possible."

"Maybe it's our spark? Or sprite power?"

He stares at me, still incredulous. "That's amazing," he says, his eyes alight.

"Or *'amazeballs'* as Liz would say," I add.

He laughs. "It's incredible, really," he says again, shaking his head in disbelief. "Are you sure? How far along are you?"

"I don't know yet, but I have a feeling it happened the first night we were together, so it could be six weeks."

He does some swift calculations. "So he would be born in April?"

"Or she."

"Or she," he smiles, "of course."

"Yes, I think so. I'll need to go to the doctor to be certain. I looked it up and April would mean a diamond birthstone. As if that means anything. I think finding out I'm pregnant is turning me a little crazy. I was already looking up names online."

He laughs. "A diamond birthstone is very fitting for your aura," he says, "clear and brilliant." He picks me up and spins us around again. "I can't believe this. We're going to have a baby."

"So you're okay with it?" I ask.

He sets me down and meets my eyes. "*Okay* with it? I'm more than okay with it. I'm amazed … and ecstatic … and delirious." He pulls me close again and plants his lips on mine. "I can't believe this," he says again, shaking his head.

I laugh. He does look quite dazed.

“Have you told anyone else yet?” he asks.

I shake my head. “I thought you should be the first.”

He smiles and in the back of my mind I picture myself trying to explain my pregnancy to my mom—I have a feeling her reaction will not be quite as thrilled as Alexander’s. Not by a long shot.

“Forget surfing, let’s go celebrate,” Alexander says, starting to take off his wetsuit.

“Wait,” I say, “I actually like the idea of just celebrating out on the water. I like sitting on our boards together and waiting for the waves with you.”

He smiles and pulls me into his embrace. “I like waiting for anything with you,” he says as he kisses me softly in the late summer sun, the sound of the breaking waves our only audience.

“There’s something I haven’t told you,” I say after we’ve finished surfing for the day and we’re sitting on our towels in our swimsuits warming ourselves in the sun. I glance over at Alexander as he runs his fingers through his wet, tousled hair and leans back on his elbows.

“You’re having twins?”

I chuckle. Our feet are next to each other in the warm sand and I nudge his foot and toss some sand at his ankle with my toes. “I could be,” I say, “for all we know. But that’s not what I’m talking about.”

“What is it?” he asks.

My eyes trail over his hard, muscled torso, noting the long, curved scar that starts under his heart and traces down over his ribs and disappears near the end of his ab muscles where his board shorts hang low on his hips. I shiver a little as I think about how Avestan's Maker, Malentus, wounded him so badly.

"It's the reason I think I might have gotten pregnant that first night we were together," I say. "I heard something."

He meets my eyes. "What do you mean?"

"As we were falling asleep that night I had a memory from when I was in the ocean. A memory of hearing my dad's voice telling me to *protect the baby, at all costs.* I thought I imagined it … it didn't even make any sense … but now that I'm pregnant I can't help but wonder if it was real."

Alexander sits up from his reclined position. "It sounds real. And, regardless, your dad is right. Our child will be unlike any other being—not a mortal or a sprite or a guardian but something else, and very powerful."

I consider his words. I like the idea of having an especially mighty baby but I also know what that could mean. "So Avestan will come after us?"

Alexander avoids the question. "Let's talk about that later," he says, "for now let's just enjoy the mind-blowing fact that we're going to be parents. We need to get you an appointment with a doctor to confirm it."

I nod. "And to make sure all's well. But what if the doctor looks in there and it has wings or something," I say. "How the heck will I explain that?"

Alexander laughs. “I don’t think that will be a problem, but you do tend to surprise, Miss Jane.”

“As do you, Mr. Ronin—the guardian who supposedly couldn’t get me pregnant.”

He laughs. “Touché. I should have realized that nothing with you is ever impossible.”

He leans over and kisses me, softly at first, and then in that way he always does that makes my knees weak and my heart swoon.

Chapter Three

It's been six days since I took the pregnancy test but I decided not to tell anyone (other than Alexander) until I could get an appointment with a doctor to confirm it. To say it's been tough being around Liz and Finn and my mom for the past few days with this secret bubbling over inside me threatening to bust out is an understatement, but somehow I've managed to hold it in and not appear suspicious. It kind of makes me wonder if I must go around looking like a grinning, anxious fool on a regular basis and apparently now is no notable exception.

Today, when Alexander accompanies me to the doctor's office for my appointment and an ultrasound confirms that we are, indeed, a little over six weeks pregnant, the way he squeezes my hand and smiles at me makes my heart glow and swell in my chest. And the look in his eyes when we see our tiny dot on the screen with a fluttering heartbeat (no wings, thank God, *at least not yet*) is something I will always remember, and cherish. Our baby may not have been planned but it is already loved beyond belief.

During the office visit, Dr. Morgan, my gynecologist, is upbeat, matter-of-fact, and she answers all my questions patiently. She advises prenatal vitamins *(already on them since I found out, thank you)*, and she says some couples choose not to announce their pregnancies broadly until twelve weeks have passed.

After we leave I consider her suggestion, but I still decide to tell my mom. And Liz and Finn, too. I don't think

I can keep the news in much longer anyway. Although I have to admit, putting it off for a while is tempting in some ways. I'm still very worried about my mom's reaction.

"Should we go tell Edwin?" I ask as we're driving away from the doctor's appointment.

"Maybe I should tell him first," Alexander says, glancing over.

"Why?" I say, "I kind of want to see his reaction. And I have questions for him."

Alexander is silent for a moment and then he nods. "Okay, we'll do it together."

When we get to Alexander's house, I'm nervous and excited and not sure what to expect in terms of Edwin's reaction. I know this news, like the realization that I was a sprite, is going to challenge his beliefs of the supposed rules and abilities governing the guardian world and I hope the accompanying surprise will be a happy one.

Edwin heats some water for tea on the stove as Alexander and I sit down in the kitchen to join him. We make chitchat until the tea's ready and then tell him we have something we want to talk with him about.

"Is everything okay?" he asks as he hands us our cups and sits down with his.

"We have some interesting and amazing news," Alexander says, eyeing Edwin carefully.

"I'm pregnant," I burst out with a broad smile. I hadn't meant to lay it on him quite like that but I can't contain it any longer.

Edwin doesn't answer. Not only that, but far from the congratulations I was expecting, he looks positively stricken. Perhaps even frightened. He sets his cup down and it clatters against the saucer.

"Is this certain?" he asks, his voice low and measured.

"Yes," Alexander and I answer together.

"And you're certain it's Alexander's?" Edwin asks me.

"*Edwin,*" Alexander says harshly.

"Yes," I say to Edwin. "I'm certain. Alexander is the only person I've ever been with."

"My apologies, but I had to ask," he says to me, looking serious … and pensive. He peers down at his hands on the table and goes silent for a long minute.

"What's going on?" I ask as I look at the both of them in turn.

"There was a story," Edwin says finally, looking up at Alexander.

"What kind of story?" I ask.

"That a baby born to a guardian would presage the final war between dark and light."

I look at Alexander. "Did you know this?"

The look on his face gives me his answer. "It's just a story," he says.

"Like the stories of sprites that we all dismissed until Declan came along," Edwin says, looking at both of us. "It was considered only a story because we all know guardians can't have progeny. Now you're telling me that Declan is pregnant, by a guardian. That changes things."

I swallow. "I thought you would be happy for us."

Edwin's eyes meet mine and he reaches across the table to touch my hand. "Declan," he says, "forgive me. Of course I'm happy for you … I'm happy for you both. But this is quite stunning news and shockwaves could reverberate far and wide. Whatever happens, we have to be prepared."

"Why?" I ask as I place my hand over my stomach protectively.

"Because," Edwin says, "a child like yours, born of a guardian and sprite, could quite simply change the world. We have to keep you and the baby safe."

We're all silent for a moment as Edwin's words sink in.

"You mean from Avestan? He'll go after an innocent child?" I ask.

"I'm saying that when Avestan finds out it will be dangerous, and if he connects the baby to Alexander he'll do everything in his power to make sure your child is never born."

As Edwin's words sink in, I look at Alexander.

"I also fear," Edwin adds, "that by attacking Malentus and stirring up that corner of the world we may have won the battle only to lose the war. And now, with a child in the mix, the stakes are higher."

His words hang heavy in the air between us.

"But if Alexander hadn't attacked Malentus," I say, "I might not have been able to save Justin from Avestan. And the fact that he's weakened now—because of what Alexander did—doesn't that help us?"

"For now," Edwin says, "but Avestan has gone to ground, in Nusquam. The dark guardians gain power from the pain and despair that permeates that realm. He knows Alexander can't follow him there and it will give him the time he needs to recover."

"Did you know that he was in Nusquam?" I ask Alexander. "That means you can't get to him before he gains his strength back—"

"It's all right," he says, putting up his hand reassuringly. "There's always another plan. If there's a silver lining, Avestan should be recovering for months. It will buy us some time, maybe even until the baby is born if we're lucky."

"And I suppose you're already formulating this new plan?" I'm unable to hold back a trace of a smile as I say the words. Alexander always has a plan. For everything.

Alexander smiles back. "Yes. I'm working on it."

"What about Alenna?" I ask. Alenna's conversion to the dark side still has me staggering. Reconciling the Alenna I knew—whose energy always seemed positive—with the woman who knocked me out and tossed me into the ocean to die has been difficult, to say the least. The image of her kissing Avestan is still seared in my mind because it shocked me so thoroughly.

"Presumably she's with Avestan," Edwin replies. "We don't know for sure."

"Was Alenna working against us all along?" I ask. "I never sensed it."

"She misled us all, Declan," Edwin answers. "Dark energy is powerful. I trusted her implicitly. We all did."

"But when did she turn?" For some reason it's important to me to identify exactly when and where my instincts went wrong.

"We can't know for certain," Edwin says.

"In hindsight," Alexander replies, "I think she may have been wavering when I came back to San Mar and she arranged for us to be seen together by Avestan. She forced the kiss and made more of it than I wanted. Afterwards she asked if there was anything left between us. She said she couldn't understand why I would want to be with a mortal, or even a sprite, over a fellow guardian. I sense now that maybe she was making a final effort before succumbing to Avestan."

"What did you say to her?"

"What I'd said before," Alexander answers, meeting my eyes. "That the love I have with her is a great love, but of friendship. And that I was sorry but I'm in love with you. And that someday she'd experience the same kind of spark we have together and she'd understand."

I nod. I know I should be angry—I mean, the woman tried to take my boyfriend away, not to mention the fact that she also tried to *kill* me—but somehow the strongest feeling I have, at the apex of my many stacked emotions, is sadness. I feel sorry for the fact that she would seek love and acceptance from someone so dark and violent as Avestan. How can she want to be with the man who brutally murdered her in her last life? How can she mistake that for love?

"I still can't conceive that if she couldn't be with you, she could find comfort with Avestan," I say, "and that she's a fallen guardian."

Edwin nods. “It was a great loss to our side. We all feel it keenly.” He looks over at Alexander.

“Did Alexander tell you about Avestan’s connection to me?” I ask Edwin.

“Yes, I was terribly sorry, Declan, to hear that Malentus had a hand in your father’s death.”

“He said there was another part to it,” I say. “That the two parts intersected.”

Edwin nods. “Alexander and I have been looking into it.”

“Have you found anything?”

“Nothing concrete,” Alexander replies. He glances over at Edwin.

“We fear the connection further involves Malentus,” Edwin says, “which would be deeply unfortunate.”

I think of the long, angry scar on Alexander’s side, a mark from Malentus, and the older scar on Alexander’s temple by his left eye, which he keeps as a reminder of Avestan, his own brother, turning against him. The fact that I have a connection to both of the dark guardians who wounded Alexander so deeply is markedly painful.

The thought of either of them coming back to exact their revenge on me, Alexander, and our baby sends a cold chill through my body. One that I know I’ll never be fully rid of unless somehow Alexander’s new plan—whatever it is—eliminates them from our lives.

For good.

Chapter Four

Um, mom, I know you always told me to use protection if I was sexually active, but ...

Uh, mom, I know I just started school but I don't think what I'm about to tell you will affect my studies or getting my degree ...

Uh, mom, I know Alexander and I just got back together recently, but you know how much we love each other and we belong together ...

Uh, mom, you know how I've always been a responsible girl? I still am, but I have some news ...

Um, hey mom, you know how you always said you looked forward to being a grandmother someday?

I'm practicing in the mirror what I'm going to say to my mom. I suggested to Alexander that I tell my mom first and then we can all talk together later because I thought she'd feel less blindsided that way. But I have no idea how best to broach the subject. I can't exactly just pop out with, 'Guess what, mom? I'm pregnant.' Or maybe that *is* the way to do it—just rip off the ol' band-aid and boom, it's done.

My mom loves Alexander, no question there. But she's been on the sidelines watching us break up twice in the last year, with no decent explanation from me either time. I suspect she chalked it up to stupidly hormonal, overly dramatic teenager stuff but I never was really like that before so maybe she just thought I was crazy.

At any rate, she has no idea that we didn't *want* to break up, we *had* to. Because we were fighting dark angels out to destroy us both and tip the world into darkness.

Which sounds totally looney tunes when you say it out loud and I can never tell her anything like that or she'll feel compelled to put me on anti-psychotic meds. So what's a girl to do?

I take a deep breath. I've been a responsible person my entire life. And my mom loves me. Those are basically my two main selling points to fall back on.

Plus the fact that my mom loves babies. So that's three main selling points, right?

Sure, keep telling yourself that, teen mom.

Oh God, I'm starting to feel faint. I have no idea how this will go.

I take a deep breath and head downstairs.

"*You didn't use protection?!*" My mom's voice is laced with incredulity. Perhaps the rip-off-the-band-aid approach was not the best choice, in retrospect.

"We were protected," I say, choosing my words carefully, "but it didn't work." *Technically true.*

My mom is silent as she stares at me for a long moment.

Please don't ask what *kind* of protection, I silently pray to myself over and over. What the heck could I say? Angels? *Please don't ask, please don't ask, please don't ask ... I don't want to lie.*

She sits down and rests her hands on the kitchen table and looks down at them. After another long moment she looks up at me again. "Declan, you and Alexander just got back together."

"I know, mom. But we're together for good now. Alexander and I love each other." I can hear how crazy teenager-y this all sounds as the words trip out of my mouth. If Alexander wasn't an angel, I'd wonder about my sanity, too. Finishing college first—and both of us having full-time jobs—would have been a measurably wiser choice before having children. I'm not too young to see it from my mom's objectively adult standpoint, but I can't explain it to her.

"You've only known Alexander a year and you've broken up twice in that time," she says quietly. "And you never really explained to me why … not entirely anyway."

I nod but don't say anything, which I'm sure is frustrating and befuddling to her. We've always been close. *I'm sorry I can't explain, mom, because if I do you'll think I'm a complete nutter, as Alexander would say.*

She meets my eyes. "I won't lie and say I don't like Alexander. I do. Very much. He's a nice boy with very kind eyes. He reminds me of your father in a lot of ways."

My heart feels hopeful. *Maybe she's coming around?*

"Have you told him?" she asks.

"Yes," I say. "Alexander's happy. Thrilled, actually."

"So you'll raise the baby together?"

"Yes, of course mom, we love each other. Alexander is a good man."

She nods. "Do you want to marry him?"

Her question takes me by surprise. I honestly hadn't even thought about marriage and that's a wonder in itself. Should I have thought about it? Alexander and I haven't discussed it. Would I marry him? Yes. Absolutely. No question. But I almost feel as though, with the connection we share, marriage is superfluous. Just a slip of paper. We're already married to each other in the way that matters to me—that string of light that connects our hearts and the way we feel when we're together, like two souls connecting *just so*.

"We haven't talked about that yet," I say, "but yes, I love Alexander. I want to be with him forever, mom." I meet her eyes and I can tell that she sees the deep truth of how I feel. The same way she felt about my dad.

She nods, her eyes getting a little misty. "You'll have to make this work with your schoolwork," she says, attempting to sound strict again but I sense that I may have won her over. "You can't let it get in the way of attaining your degree."

I nod. "I know, mom. I feel the same. I'll make it work. You know I'm responsible." I can't resist throwing that last bit in, my final ace in the hole.

She's silent again for a long moment as she searches my eyes. Then she takes a deep breath and stands up. "Then if you're happy, I'm happy. There are still plenty of details to work through but I can't say I'm not thrilled at the thought of having a grandchild to dote over." She smiles and walks over to where I'm standing at the kitchen island and gives me a hug and I can tell by the way she holds me and the love that I feel from her that she meant every word she said. The fact that she didn't say something like, "We'll make the best of it," as if it was some terrible burden, means a lot to me. She's happy for me, and even thrilled a little for herself, and that takes an enormous weight off my heart.

"Thanks, mom," I say as I hug her back just as tightly. "I'm so glad you're with me on this."

She holds me by the shoulders and meets my eyes. "I'm always with you," she says with a fierceness only a mother can deliver. "No matter what. Your mom always has your back."

I smile and my eyes get watery and a lump forms in my throat. "Thanks, mom."

"I just can't believe I'm going to be a grandmother … my baby is having a baby," she says with amazement as she places her hand on my stomach. "How far along are you?"

"A little over six weeks."

"Have you already been to the doctor?"

I nod.

"Okay, we need to get you on prenatal vitamins and make a list of what you can and can't eat … oh, and we should get you that book, *What to Expect When you're Expecting* … and we'll need to start a registry of things you'll need for the baby and …"

And with that, my mom has not only accepted my news, she's off and running doing what she does best: taking good care of everyone in her sunshiny orbit.

Chapter Five

I'm sitting on the outside deck at A-plus Coffee on the UCSM campus waiting for Liz and Finn. The campus is only a two-mile bike ride from my house but it's up on a hill with sweeping views of San Mar all the way to the ocean. I take a deep breath, drinking in the picture-perfect vista laid out in front of me. I love it here. Not just for the atmosphere but because I can finally call myself a college student, which, I must admit, is pretty great. I feel like a real adult finally. My world feels so much bigger than it ever did in high school. Bigger and full of possibility.

"Hey, look who's here," says a voice behind me.

I turn around to see Justin Wright, my friend and former co-worker at Fields and Morris L.L.C. This is only the second time I've seen him since we were both nearly killed by Avestan and Alenna during our supposedly innocent whale watching trip with Burt Fields—who turned out to be a cold-blooded murderer himself. Of course Justin has no memory of any of it, thank God. I almost envy him.

"Justin," I say with surprise. "How are you?"

He sits down with his coffee. "I'm good," he says with a nod. "Hey, I've been wanting to talk with you. Have you heard about everything that's been going on at Fields and Morris?"

He's referring to all the articles that have been in the local newspaper about the embezzlement fraud discovered after Burt Fields' accidental death out on the firm's yacht.

Justin doesn't realize that I'm the one who set the whole thing in motion by sending the evidence of the fraud to the other law partners anonymously.

"I know," I say, "it's been all over the news."

"Mr. Fields seemed like a decent guy. It's hard to believe."

"I guess you never know about people," I say.

He nods. "What's that saying? Who knows what darkness lies in the hearts of men?"

What an understatement. The truth of his words strikes me hard, yet again. I think about Alenna falling to be with Avestan, and I can't help thinking about Burt also, and how he comforted our family after my dad's death. Now I realize that either guilt was driving him or, worse, it was cold calculation meant to deflect any suspicion, or maybe a way to search our house for my dad's files. No matter what, it sickens me. I've run the facts through endlessly in my mind and I decided not to tell my mom the whole truth. I want to shield her from the fury and anguish that the knowledge brings. Finding out her beloved husband spent his last moments fighting for his life against a friend who betrayed him would only bring fresh pain at a time when she finally seems to be healing. I know that all too well. And the hard truth is, nothing can be done about it anyway. They're both gone now and we can't go back in time. As desperately as I'd like to.

"So how do you like college so far?" Justin asks.

"I love it," I say, happy to distract myself with a more pleasant topic. "It's so much better than high school. I love everything about it."

He laughs. "Most people are complaining about the workload this many weeks in."

I shake my head. "Nah, I can handle the work. But riding my bike up and down all these ginormous hills is what's killing me. I thought I was in good shape but maybe I need a bike with more gears." I love my beach cruiser but it only has three gears, a limitation I never even noticed was a problem until now.

"Give it another month," he says with a smile. "Your butt will be granite."

I laugh.

"You still back with the sweet boyfriend?" he asks.

"Yes. Alexander goes to school here now, too."

He nods. "I'm seeing someone new."

"You are? That's great."

"Her name is Sara and believe it or not she likes Lucky Charms for dinner."

"She's lying," I laugh. "Because she likes you."

"Well, either she likes Lucky Charms or she likes me enough to lie about it. Either way I think I'm good." He flashes a broad smile.

I chuckle. "So what else have you been up t—"

"*There* she is." I hear Liz's voice over my right shoulder and I turn to see her and Finn walking toward us, holding hands. Liz's hair is in two dark mini buns pinned on either side of the top of her head like cute panda ears. Her bangs, which used to be bright pink, are now a cool shade of blue that suits her just as well. She's wearing skinny jeans and a t-shirt that says "SOME CRAPPY BAND" in giant block letters. Finn looks cute, as usual, in jeans, a t-shirt and his favorite Volcom hoodie, which he once told me he likes to wear because "it's like a blanket you can wear outside the house." His tousled brown hair is partially covering his boyish face and I can't help noticing that it looks artfully mussed, which is hysterical because I know for a fact it's the result of him getting out of the shower and doing absolutely *nothing* to it. He insists that if you get a decent haircut on a regular schedule, hair grooming products beyond shampoo and conditioner are an unnecessary marketing scam. I don't think he even combs it other than running his fingers through it. One of the reasons he's so loyal to his hairdresser, a nice lady named Marcella, is because she told him he's right—for his hair, anyway. He has an appointment scheduled on Marcella's books every six weeks into perpetuity.

I make introductions when they arrive at our table and Justin and Liz remind me that they met once over the summer when she picked me up from work. The deck is crowded with people and there are only three chairs so Justin stands up to relinquish his. "I have to go to class anyway," he says. "But it was nice meeting you, Finn, and nice to see you again, Liz. Hope to see you both again."

"He still likes you," Liz whispers conspiratorially after he's out of earshot.

I shake my head. "He has a new girlfriend."

"They're not mutually exclusive," pipes in Finn. "You can have a girlfriend and also be attracted to someone else."

Liz's head swivels to face Finn as if it's been yanked on a spring-loaded lever. "You mean that girl Sonja in your photography class? I *knew* it. I could tell she had a thing for you when she asked you how many miles you ride on your bike per we—"

"What are you talking about?" Finn interjects. His expression is utter confusion.

"You have a girlfriend," Liz says matter-of-factly, "that would be *me* … and you just said you can have a girlfriend and also be attracted to someone else."

"I said they're not mutually exclusive," he explains. "My mom gets *People Magazine*—just take a look at the cover story almost every week. And who are you even talking about?"

"The blonde girl who asked to see your zoom lens," Liz says as her eyes narrow. "Which I'm realizing now was probably a euphemism so it's even worse than I thought. In fact, I'm getting madder by the second that she—"

He shakes his head dismissively. "I would never hand over my zoom lens … it's far too valuable."

I stifle a laugh as I watch them. It's like they're having two different conversations. I'm not sure Finn even realizes they're arguing.

"You seriously have no idea who I'm talking about?" Liz asks.

He shakes his head again, his expression persuasively blank.

Liz turns to me, the wind released from her sails. "It's redonkulous. He has no clue when girls are flirting with him."

I laugh. "You have no clue either," I say. "That guy Greg from your bio class who wanted you to be his lab partner—"

She waves her hand, cutting me off. "I knew he wanted me. I shut that down quick and told him I have a boyfriend." She looks at Finn and he responds with a satisfied smile.

"In evolutionary terms," Finn says, "it makes sense that seeking out new partners is optimal because it results in more offspring. But, for me, I've found that having a girlfriend who makes me happy means I don't notice other women in that way. That's probably why I have no idea who this girl is that you're talking about."

Liz shakes her head and smiles at him. "You know, you're unintentionally romantic—like Spock but with a very sweet marshmallow center."

I laugh because Liz could almost be describing herself. She and Finn are so different but also alike. Like a Venn diagram with just the right amount of overlap.

"I have no idea what that means," Finn replies.

She laughs and leans over to give him a kiss. "You had me at *evolutionary,* Finn. Just go with it. I love the way you think."

Chapter Six

"Do I need to get dressed up?"

Alexander is in my room. We agreed to meet at my house after my shift at Jack's Burger Shack so we can go out. Where we're going is a surprise. Right now I'm still in my red Jack's "Home of the Hula Burger" t-shirt and my favorite worn jeans and I don't know what to change into.

"Just wear whatever's comfortable. Whatever's quick."

He seems oddly nervous but I take note that he's dressed fairly casually in low slung jeans and a white button-down shirt with the sleeves rolled up to reveal his strong forearms. His tall, athletic frame makes him look like a male model, but honestly he looks like one no matter what he has on—or *not*, I can't help but think with a smile. There's a reason all those girls at San Mar High used to call him the Aussie Adonis. But we must not be going anywhere fancy because he always wears a suit when we're doing something special. He's dressed too casual for that. "Okay," I say, "but I smell like a giant French fry."

He smiles and wraps his arms around me, pulling me tight against him. "I like French fries."

I laugh as I look up into his crinkling green eyes. "At least let me take a quick shower first."

He pulls me closer until his lips are only a breath away. "Only if I can get in the shower with you." He smiles mischievously and his voice is low in the way that always makes me swoony.

I swallow hard. "My mom is home," I whisper. But my words hold little conviction. My knees go seriously weak whenever Alexander talks in that husky voice of his. And the look he's giving me right now is so hot I honestly think my bones are melting.

He kisses me—softly at first, and then like he means it, the way I love—and the kiss goes on and on until I couldn't care less if the entire population of San Mar was right here in the room with us. All that exists when he kisses me like this is the two of us and the feel of his hands pulling me close against his body and his tongue caressing mine. When Alexander pulls away, leaving me breathless, he smiles teasingly. "Well, if your mom is home, I guess we'll have to save this for later. I'll wait downstairs."

I push his arm and he chuckles before he walks out and closes the door. *Was he serious?* I wait for him to come back and when he doesn't I walk into the bathroom still in a daze and smile as I strip off my clothes and step under the hot spray of the shower and let out a soft sigh. *God, I love my boyfriend.* I can't help but daydream about "later" as I enjoy the feel of the water pouring over me.

After my shower I decide on a simple blue sundress that my mom once said matches my eyes and I lay out a white sweater wrap to bring along in case it gets cold. As I look in the mirror one last time to check my appearance, I touch the necklace Alexander gave me for my birthday. It's a dainty sterling silver heart, engraved on the back with "A.R. + D.J. Always." I haven't taken it off since he gave it to me a few weeks ago and took me on another memorable flight around the world the night I turned nineteen. I can't help thinking that this year will be a seminal one for us. For one year—and one year only—Alexander and I will be the same age. After this I'll keep getting older and Alexander will stay the same.

Don't worry about any of that for now.

I repeat this message to myself, as I have so many times before. What's that saying about just living in the moment? The problem is, eventually the future *becomes* the moment, and what do you do then? I take a deep breath and push all those thoughts to the side, distracting myself by fussing with my hair a little until I settle on putting it up into a soft bun and tugging out a few golden tendrils to frame my face. Then I apply a little mascara and some lip gloss and I'm ready to go. When I walk downstairs I find Alexander standing at the kitchen island chatting with my mom and, to my surprise, Chief Stephens. I know the chief keeps telling me to call him Mark now that he's sort of dating my mom, but I've known him so long as the Chief of Police that it takes an extra mental kick to remember to call him by his first name.

Alexander smiles wide when he sees me. "You look gorgeous," he whispers in my ear in a way that makes my heart flutter as he puts his arm around me and tugs me in close.

"Hi Mark," I say to Chief Stephens, proud of myself for not stumbling over his name. "You and my mom have plans tonight?"

"Mark stopped by to fix the doohickey that broke in the dishwasher," my mom says. "I mentioned it to him and apparently he's very handy."

"I'm good with doohickeys," Mark says wryly and my mother meets his eyes and laughs.

"Well I don't know what it's called," she trills as she lightly pushes his arm.

Holy wowza. Judy Jane is being flirty. This is monumental progress on the dating front.

"You know, Mrs. Jane, you can always call on me to do any repairs you need, too," Alexander says. I immediately step on his foot and he looks at me, his eyes flashing momentary confusion.

"But I don't think Alexander knows a lot about dishwashers," I say. "So thank you, Mark, for helping us."

"My pleasure," says Mark and then he glances over at my mom and smiles. Suddenly I feel like I'm the parent watching two high school kids who are dating. It's cute. And weird.

"Well," I announce, feeling a little awkward, "Alexander and I are going out so I guess we'll see you guys later. Mom, I stopped at the store on my way home from work and got you the bread you wanted. It's in the pantry."

"Thanks, sweetie," she says and she comes over and gives me a hug and then she hugs Alexander too, for good measure. "Have fun tonight, kids." She kisses us both on the cheek.

"Thanks mom," I say. Then I call out loudly to Mark as we leave, "Have fun fixing my mom's doohickey." Only after the words are out of my mouth do I realize how oddly wrong and pornographic that sounds. I look over at Alexander when we get outside.

"Have fun fixing my mom's doohickey?" he repeats back to me and we both burst out laughing.

"Now I get why you didn't want me to offer any repairs," he adds.

"She insists they're not dating but did you see her touch his arm? That was definitely flirty, right?"

"Let me put it this way," he says, "I remember the first time you touched my arm like that."

"We're going up on the mountain?" I ask delightedly when Alexander turns on the back road leading into Redwood Park.

"Close," he says.

When we park and get out of the car he stands in front of me looking nervous again. "I think I should carry you in," he says.

I shrug, "Okay." Why get sweaty if I don't have to?

He raises me into his arms as if it's no more effort than lifting a pencil. "When we get close, cover your eyes."

I smile. "Yes, sir."

He laughs. "Do you remember the last time I carried you in here?" he asks as he begins walking down the forest path.

"Yes, but you held me like a sack of potatoes that time."

"And your dress rode up to show off your knickers as I remember," he laughs, "so I switched and held you like this."

"Like the gentleman angel you are," I say with a smile. "Are we going to the fairy ring?"

"Yes."

"Where we first kissed," I say with a happy sigh. "Of course I remember."

He smiles. "How's the baby doing? Are you comfortable?"

"Considering he's the size of a lentil bean at this point, I think we're doing okay."

He chuckles. "*He?*"

"I'm using it as an interchangeable universal pronoun. It's too much work to keep saying 'he or she' all the time. And 'it' just seems blatantly wrong."

He plants a kiss on my lips. "I love you."

"Ditto."

He keeps walking and as we get closer to the fairy ring he seems nervous again. "Are you feeling good about us?" he asks.

"Of course," I say, starting to get a little worried, "aren't you?"

"Long term I mean."

"Yes, long term. Is something wrong?"

He sets me down, facing him, when we reach the ring.

"That's good to hear," he says.

He rolls his shoulders, straightening his shirt, and he seems nervous. When he doesn't say anything else I fill the silence. "Is it okay if I turn around now?"

He swallows. "Yes."

I turn around and my hand flutters to my chest as I gasp. Alexander has decorated the fairy ring the same way he did the night of our first kiss, from the blue and white lights in the trees to the sparkling silver hearts surrounding our carved initials bathed in a sunbeam coming down from the sky. There's a blanket laid out with a cooler, and all the memories I have of how it felt to kiss Alexander for the first time flood over me. He steps in front of me and takes my hand and I look at him with misty eyes.

"It's beautiful," I say softly.

"You're beautiful," he says as he leads me over to where our initials are carved. The sun shines down like a sentry on the remains of the redwood that helped form this beautiful ring of stately, towering trees. As I watch with amazement and emotions overflowing, Alexander bends down on one knee. And with my heart beating like a hummingbird's wings, I listen as he begins to speak words that I know come from his heart.

"Declan, you know how much I love you," he says as tears well up in my eyes. "I felt your goodness the first day I sat next to you in Mr. Brody's homeroom class and you blushed. I love that you always manage to make me laugh," he says with a smile, "when I don't expect it, or when things are going wrong—in fact, *especially* when things are going wrong. And the way you smile, with your lips a little crooked in that cute way of yours, and that brilliant light in your sea-blue eyes … I once joked with you about getting lost in my eyes, when the truth is I get lost in yours every time I look in them. But your beauty on the outside, which takes my breath away every time I see you, isn't even close to being the most beautiful thing about you. Your kindness, to everyone who crosses your path, and your compassion, and empathy … and the way you feel about your friends and how you stand by them. And even the way your power comes out when your heart's involved. I'm looking at your aura right now and it's so strikingly beautiful it makes my heart literally vibrate—in a good way," he adds, and I let out a laugh with tears in my eyes, "and it reflects what's inside you, what I've always seen … and felt. You're the soul that makes mine hum and the woman I love and who I hope to be with, for this life and every life, for eternity. So Declan Jane, will you marry me? And make me the happiest guardian in the universe?"

I smile, eyes blurry with tears. "Yes," I say, nodding and laughing and nodding some more, overwhelmed, "*yes.*"

He slips his hand in his pocket and slides out a ring and holds it up between his finger and thumb. It's a beautifully intricate platinum band that splits into two at the sides to hold a large, square setting of a vivid blue topaz surrounded by an array of small, stunningly clear diamonds. "I almost forgot this," he says with a laugh and I see his eyes filling with emotion. He holds my hand in his and slips it on my ring finger. "Inspired by your aura."

"It's beautiful," I breathe as I meet his eyes, tears overflowing. He stands and I wrap my arms around him and he kisses me, ardently, and I return his kiss with all the love in my heart.

We pause and smile into each other's eyes for what feels as though it could never be long enough, treasuring the moment. "I want you to know that I planned this, always," Alexander says. "I just never imagined you'd get pregnant before I had a chance to ask."

"Wait," I say wryly, "you expect me to believe that you, Alexander Ronin, had a plan?"

He laughs. "The only thing I didn't plan was how nervous I'd be."

"I sensed that," I laugh. "Until you knelt down I couldn't figure out why. But I love that you were nervous."

"You love that I was terrified you'd say no?"

"You can't have thought I'd say no?"

"You're very unpredictable, Miss Jane."

I smile. "As are you, Mr. Ronin. You surprised me tonight. Very happily. Not asking me to get dressed up—or even telling me I should *shower*—was a clever ruse that left me entirely unsuspecting. Although I could have ended up smelling like French fries and Hula Burgers when you proposed, and for that I would never forgive you."

He laughs. "It was a bold risk, I'll grant you."

"That being said," I say with a smile, "I'll marry you on two conditions."

"And those are?"

"First, that we have a small ceremony, here, with just family and close friends."

"My thoughts exactly. And?"

"Second, that we make love, right now, on that picnic blanket."

He laughs out loud. "It's like you're reading my mind," he says as he sweeps me into his arms and carries me over to the blanket where we do just that.

And, just like always, it's magical, and beautiful, and too sweet to express with words.

Chapter Seven

"I have some news," I say to Finn and Liz as we sit on the cliffs overlooking the ocean. We rode our bikes here because it's such a beautiful day and we haven't hung out in a while. Between work, school, and everything else we all have going on, it's been hard to see each other as much as we used to.

"Let me guess, you walked in on your mom and the chief doing, shall we say, *police maneuvers?*" Liz says.

"No," I say, pushing her arm and laughing. "Why are you so fixated on that? You kill me."

"I don't know," Liz says, "I keep picturing Chief Stephens telling your mom she's under arrest for stealing his heart and it cracks me up, what can I say?"

I look over at Finn for support but he just shakes his head. "I don't want to think about your mom's sex life," he says flatly.

"Hear, hear," I say in hearty agreement as I look at Liz who just grins at me.

"All right, all right," she says, with her best put-upon tone, "I'll give you a reprieve from all police-related innuendo. For now, anyway. It's just that it's too easy … what with how sweet and proper they both are … and then you add the uniform, the paraphernalia, the way they frisk people … the jokes are like ripe fruit, just dangling there, waiting to be picked off, one by one." She looks at me and

I smile and shake my head. "All right," she laughs, "so what's your news?"

I can't hold it in anymore. My face beams as I thrust out my hand in front of both of them to show off my engagement ring.

"You got a new ring?" says Finn, looking confused and seriously underwhelmed.

"No, Finn, for God's sake," Liz cries out, "it's an engagement ring. She's getting married!" She jumps up to hug me.

"And that's not all," I say as I hug them both, smiling and laughing. "I'm pregnant."

Liz freezes. "You're joking," she says, eyes wide.

"No," I say, shaking my head. "I really am."

"Holy *Scheisse*," she says under her breath, staring at me dumbfounded. She's taken to swearing in German lately.

Finn just looks at me with his mouth open. "You're *pregnant*?" he says finally.

"I feel like this calls for a joke," Liz says, "involving Chief Stephens and police shotguns and weddings but I'm actually speechless."

I smile and push her arm. "It's not a shotgun wedding. Alexander and I want to be married and by some twist of fate I also got pregnant."

I glance over at Finn, who's still staring at me. "You're experiencing a lot of life's typical milestones in a compressed timeframe," he comments, obviously recovered from his initial shock.

I can't help thinking he's right. It's as if everything accelerated since I met Alexander—like we're racing ahead of something, but I'm not sure what. "I was surprised at first," I say, "like you guys are, but I'm thrilled now, and so is Alexander and I hope you guys are thrilled, too." I pat my stomach. "You're going to be this baby's auntie and uncle you know."

Liz's eyes well up. "Of *course* we're thrilled for you … oh my God. You just threw me there for a minute. And it takes a lot to throw me … I can't believe I'm going to be an auntie! And Finn, you're going to be an uncle." She gets choked up as she continues. "And this is our only chance, you know … you're the closest thing to a real sister either of us will ever have."

I meet her eyes and get a little choked up myself as we all hug in a big, mushy group. "As far as I'm concerned," I say, "you *are* my real sister and brother—we just happen to have different parents."

"That makes no sense," Finn says, shaking his head.

Liz and I laugh and we all hug some more as she studies the ring again and asks for more details.

In this happy moment, thoughts of dark guardians and danger are pushed so far back in my mind I feel as if nothing could ever go wrong.

My mom got teary when I told her about Alexander's proposal. She was thrilled, of course, and has been pushing me to let her help plan the wedding ever since. I'm at twelve weeks now, officially into my second trimester and it's starting to feel more real by the day. The only problem with my mom helping to plan the wedding is that there isn't much to plan. I want our wedding to be simple and private with only me, Alexander, Edwin, my mom (I told her to also invite Mark, and I hope she does), plus Liz and Finn and their families. Edwin wants to perform the ceremony, and we'll have some champagne, sparkling water, and maybe some hors d'oeuvres and that's pretty much it. Easy peasy, right? Alexander is handling the decorations and he joked that I won't need "something old" (that's him and his many lives) or "something blue" (because I have my aura). That just leaves something new (which I guess we could count as the baby—you don't get much newer than that) and something borrowed, which I'll have to figure out. Oh, and the bouquet, which I already decided I want to be a simple mixture of blue and white forget-me-nots, like the bouquet of flowers Alexander had waiting for me in the cabin the night we made love for the first time. And of course my dress, which I also want to be fairly simple and unadorned. My mom and I have been going to bridal stores all morning with no luck so far. Now we're at the third one and I'm hoping the third time's the charm.

"You don't like any of these?" my mom asks, as we flip through the racks.

"They're pretty, but I don't want anything so elaborate. I just want it to be simple. And these prices are *nutballs*," I say in a hushed tone, showing her the tag on the heavily-beaded dress in front of me. "I paid less for Archie than this one costs." Out of the corner of my eye I notice the bridal consultant, who's been oddly snobbish since we came in, flash a look of disapproval. My mom and I must not look like big spenders and I guess I just proved it.

"Things have changed since I got married," my mom whispers back. "I think people spend more now on weddings than your father and I did on our first *house*." She looks around at all the beaded, buttoned, intricately lacey, embellished dresses throughout the store. "Maybe these bridal stores aren't the right place for us if you're looking for something simple."

"Maybe we should go to some regular stores," I suggest. "I was picturing something that looks more like a white sundress. Kind of flowy but casual."

"You mean like *my* wedding dress?"

I realize the minute my mom says it that, yes, I *have* been imagining a dress like hers. I shake off dusty, forgotten memories of flipping through her wedding album as a little girl and the remembered photographs flow to the forefront of my brain. "I can't believe I didn't think of it," I say, "but yes, exactly like yours. Maybe that's where I got the idea, subconsciously."

She smiles. "Well I know a place that has one exactly like mine."

"Where?"

"It's called the Jane's attic."

"You still have it?"

"Of course. It didn't occur to me to suggest you wear it. I assumed you'd want a classic dress. Your dad and I had a simple wedding, too."

"Do you think it would fit?" I ask.

"I know it will. You're a little shorter than me but we could have it hemmed. And it could count as your 'something borrowed.' Do you really think you might like to wear it?"

"I think I'd *love* to wear it."

She smiles and pulls me in for a tight hug and plants a kiss on my cheek. "Then let's go have a nice mother-daughter lunch. Then we can finish our shopping in The Jane's Attic, San Mar's newest vintage bridal shop."

"Can you tell me again how you and Dad met?"

I ask the question as I eat another bite of my surprisingly delicious quinoa, barley, and farro salad at Sweet Pea's Café downtown. "I know you always say it was love at first sight. But was that really it? You just knew?"

"It *was* love at first sight—for both of us—that part is true," my mom answers, "and I honestly didn't even believe in love at first sight until it happened to me. But the other part, which your dad used to prefer I skip over, was that for some reason, probably related to being born male, he took a heckuva long time coming around."

I laugh. "What do you mean?"

"Well, I first saw him my senior year of college. He was a transfer student and I saw him on campus one day and our eyes met and, I don't know, Declan, something in me just leapt at the sight of him. It was like he literally sparkled, above the rest."

I smile. I love the look in my mom's eyes when she talks about my dad. I imagine her aura right now as bright, cheery, yellow and white sunbeams shining out from her in all directions.

"I knew he felt something too," she continues, "because he smiled at me. And the *way* he smiled at me—with this look in his eyes …" Her voice drifts off and she stares for a moment and takes a deep breath with a faraway smile at the memory. "I just *knew,*" she says, "there's no other way to explain it."

"So you started dating and that was that?"

"Well, that's how your father preferred I tell it," she says, "but the truth is, he kept me guessing—and frustrated—for such a long time I almost gave up on him."

"Really? Why?"

"The day I first saw him I ended up running into him again later at the Student Union, and he walked up and introduced himself and he said—" my mom pauses and smiles again and practically giggles with that faraway look in her eyes before continuing, "I'll never forget it, Declan, he was so handsome and he had these deep, brilliant blue eyes and he walked up and said, *'I think I need to know you.'*" She stops talking for a moment and smiles again, remembering, and she instantly looks twenty years younger.

"What did you say?" I ask, transfixed by her story. She's never given me these details before.

"Well, we started talking, and we ended up talking for hours—he was so witty and smart—and we just *clicked.* And then we started dating, or what I assumed was dating, but he frustrated me because he wouldn't make a move. He insisted we were friends. And we *were* friends—we became such good friends. *Best* friends, really. We had such a connection." She peers off into the distance for a moment with a faint smile of remembrance before continuing. "But Declan, you probably don't want to hear this about your parents, but I knew we weren't *just* friends … the way he looked at me … let's just say there was definitely more than just friendly feelings between us."

I chuckle. I love it when my mom talks to me like I'm one of her girlfriends. "So what did you do?"

"My friend Kim convinced me I needed to make the first move—to show him I was interested in being more than just friends, in case he wasn't sure. So I mustered up the courage to finally do it the next time we saw each other."

"And? What happened?" I ask, on the edge of my seat.

"He turned away! I was so embarrassed. And mad, to be honest. I told myself that was it—he was either leading me on or I'd read it wrong and he wasn't interested. I honestly didn't know what to make of it, but I decided I couldn't go on seeing him if all he wanted was friendship because I wanted so much more. I refused to see him anymore after that and I started dating this other guy, Malcolm, who'd been pursuing me. I thought maybe it would help me get over your dad."

"What? Who's Malcolm? How come I never heard any of this before?" I had no idea my mom dated someone else after dating my dad. The story I had in my mind was that my mom and dad saw each other, fell in love, and that was it—*boom*—happily ever after. It's fascinating to hear that it was far more complicated than that.

"Your dad never liked me to mention him … because of what happened."

"What happened?" I ask, thoroughly intrigued.

"Your father saw me with Malcom one day. We were holding hands and I think we may have been getting ready to go away for the weekend, if I remember right. Anyway, the next thing I knew—I think it was a few days later, I can never remember the timing—your father was at my apartment door, looking like hell, and he professed his love for me and took me in his arms and kissed me. He asked me to marry him, right then and there, and I knew it was crazy but I said yes."

I smile. How romantic. And a little crazy and spontaneous, too—like straight out of a rom-com. I never knew how precarious my mom's and dad's romance was—it's funny to think that if they hadn't both been slightly nutso to the same degree, I might not be here.

"And the rest is history," she says with a choked-up flourish of her hands as her eyes get misty. She remains silent for a long moment, looking down. "God, I miss him, Declan," she says in a whisper as she wipes away a tear, "*so much.*"

"I know, mom," I say, my eyes welling up along with hers. "Me, too." I reach over to touch her arm and she squeezes my hand.

"I felt like he spoke to me the other day, though," she says through a tear-stained smile.

"Really?" My spine tingles a little at her words. I never shared with my mom that I imagined I heard my dad speaking to me, too.

She nods. "Mark came over for dinner and after he left I was sitting in bed reading and I was starting to doze off and suddenly, I swear to you, I felt like your dad was right there next to me, where he always used to be, and he said, clear as day, *'it's okay.'*" Fresh tears start to fall and she wipes them away and looks around the outside patio to see if anyone is watching us. "Then he said it again," she says. "He whispered: *'I'll always love you, my beautiful ray of sunlight. And it's okay.'*" She wipes away more tears. "That's what he used to call me, his *beautiful ray of sunlight*. I'd almost forgotten."

I wipe away fresh tears of my own. "What do you think it meant?"

"I think he's trying to tell me it's okay to move on."

I nod, teary-eyed. "I think so, too, mom."

"Mark's a good man," she says, regaining her composure and smoothing her napkin in her lap.

"He is," I say. "I like him."

She looks up. "You do?"

"Of course, mom, I'm the one that encouraged you to go out with him in the first place. He's a nice guy. A *good* guy."

She nods. "He told me he's falling in love with me."

"He did?"

"Yes," she smiles, her eyes bright, "and we haven't even kissed yet."

"You haven't even *kissed* him yet?" My eyes are wide as saucers. "In all this time?"

"No," she laughs, her eyes still wet, "he said he's willing to wait for me, until I'm ready."

"*Wow.*" I shake my head slowly. "That is one seriously patient man … a man who is clearly already hopelessly in love with you."

She smiles and wipes her eyes again.

"How do *you* feel?" I ask. "About him?"

She pauses and takes a deep breath and looks down, smoothing the napkin in her lap again several times before answering. "I feel like my heart is open again," she says as she looks up and meets my eyes. "And I think I'm ready."

I smile and can't help thinking that that's exactly what my dad wanted. There's no question in my mind anymore that he's watching over us.

And maybe now my dad can be at peace, and he can move on, too.

Chapter Eight

My mom pulls the opaque plastic bin from a high shelf in the attic. "Here it is," she says with a measure of satisfaction. "Let's take it to my room before we open it."

When we get to her room, she sets the bin on the bed and my heart beats a little faster as she snaps open the lid. "I had it cleaned before I stored it away," she says as she lifts out her wedding dress and holds it lovingly draped over her arms for me.

"It's beautiful," I say, reaching out to touch the soft, flowy fabric.

"I think it will fit you perfectly," she says as she lays it down on the bed and lifts another item out of the bin. It's a white, woven flower crown and as soon as I see it my heart stops mid-beat with amazement.

The fabric flowers are delicate white forget-me-nots.

I lift it and turn it over in my hand. The woven ring is so simple and beautiful, it looks like something a wood nymph would wear—utterly perfect for a wedding held in a fairy ring of stately trees. "Oh, mom, this is beautiful, too. It's perfect. Can we look at your wedding album?" I've been struggling to recall the long-ago photos that I haven't looked at since I was a little girl.

She smiles as I lay down the flower crown next to her dress. "Of course," she says as she disappears into her closet and emerges with the album in her hand.

We both sit down on the edge of her bed and open the album between us on our laps. The first photo is of my mom and dad sharing a kiss on the beach.

"We had such a simple wedding," she says as we flip through the pages, "I didn't want anything fancy and your dad and I were broke college students." She laughs. "Your dad had no family alive and my father had passed a few years earlier and my mom didn't approve of me getting married—not at first anyway—so it was just us and a bunch of our friends from school. It was more like a casual party than a typical wedding."

"Why didn't grandma approve?" I ask. I never really knew my grandmother. She died when I was very little.

"We married so spontaneously she thought I'd lost my mind and that Frank and I were both fools. But when you came along, very soon after," she says with a smile, "my mom quickly came around, too. You were irresistible."

I smile and stare at the picture of my mom walking down the aisle barefoot—if you can call the stretch of sand between where her and my dad's friends stood on the beach an aisle. She looks like a beautiful waif, with her hair down and the woven ring of flowers worn like a crown over her golden, flowing waves. In the photo, the backless white cotton sundress has a softly rounded halter neckline that scoops just enough in front to show the graceful slope of her shoulder bones, and it ties at the back of her neck. The dress gathers gently at the waist with a built-in sash and then flows to the ground. It's all soft and airy and my mom looks like a cross between a '60s love child and a sandy mirage. She's radiant and naturally beautiful and it's exactly what I pictured for myself. I'm getting married in a

Redwood fairy ring after all, so why not wear a white, flowing fairy dress and a crown of flowers?

"Mom, you were so beautiful," I say softly. I turn the page to see my dad holding her hands as they take their vows. He's barefoot also, dressed in jeans and a white button-down shirt.

"I told you we were poor," my mom says with a laugh. "Your dad didn't even own a suit. I told him I didn't care what he wore as long as he was there."

We flip slowly through the rest of the pages and my mom takes a deep breath when we're finished and closes the album and remains quiet for a moment. Then she takes another deep breath, perks herself up, and looks at me with a smile in her eyes. "Are you ready to try the dress on?" she asks.

I nod eagerly.

I strip to my underwear and she helps me slip the dress over my head and tie it at the neck. Then my mom stands behind me, beaming, as I look at my reflection in the full-length mirror on the door of her closet. "The good news is, it's adjustable," my mom says as she tugs gently on the two ends of the built-in sash at my waist and ties it behind me. "So when you start showing more, you can simply tie it looser. And we can hem it a little, too."

I smile, barely hearing her because I'm transfixed at the image in the mirror. I adore this dress. It's exactly what I envisioned. Maybe better, if that's even possible.

"Take out your ponytail," my mom says and I pull out the elastic band and shake my hair out over my shoulders. My mom arranges the hair around my face with her fingers and continues primping here and there along its lengths until I have golden waves that look natural and effortless, just the way I envisioned. Then she reaches over and places the woven crown of sparse, delicate forget-me-nots on my head, set slightly back like a headband, and it completes the look so perfectly that my eyes well up.

"Do you like it?" my mom asks.

I turn around to face her. "Mom, I *love* it," I say. "I love the crown and I love the dress. I love it all so much that I think I'm going to cry all over everything so you'd better get me some tissues."

She laughs and hands me the box from her bedside table and then hugs me tight. "You look so beautiful, sweetie. My heart is literally overflowing. I love that you want to wear the dress I wore on the happiest day of my life."

I beam up at her.

"Besides the day you were born of course," she adds.

I choke out a laugh through my tears. "I can't stop crying," I say with a smile as I dab my eyes with tissues. "Probably because of all the pregnancy hormones, according to that book you gave me."

"Oh, just wait until the third trimester," she laughs. "You'll be sobbing over hams at the supermarket."

She hugs me as I laugh and cry in her arms and think about how happy I am right now, and how incredibly happy I'll be on the day I marry Alexander … and every day afterwards to come.

But in a small back corner of my mind, one I've been desperately trying to keep contained, I know that Avestan is coming back. And possibly bringing someone worse.

And all this happiness I'm feeling could vanish in an instant.

Because the driving objective behind the dark, malevolent force of energy headed our way will be to ensure that our baby is never born and my wedding to Alexander—this wedding that I'm preparing for with so much love in my heart and hope for the future—never happens.

Chapter Nine

"You sure you don't want to get married sooner?" asks Alexander as he strips off his t-shirt. "Like tomorrow?"

I laugh as I meet his smiling eyes. I'm in his room and he just got back from running. I came here to meet him after my last class so we can go out to eat but the sight of his bare chest and his shorts hanging low on his hips and the sheer male scent of his sweat is making me want to tear off the rest of his clothes and forget about eating altogether. I shake my head to clear it and try to respond to his question.

"I like the idea of waiting until March, the first day of spring," I say. "Like a new beginning. Growing a new life together."

"In Australia," he says with an irresistible smirk, "spring is in September."

I smile. "Yes, I realize, Professor Ronin, that the vernal equinox and autumnal equinox are switched in the northern and southern hemispheres. But I like that it's still an equinox, where almost everywhere in the world gets equal time for day and night. It's balanced."

"You've put a lot of thought into this," he says.

"You're not the only one who plans things."

He smiles. "The student has become the master," he says with a laugh and I pick up his sock off the floor and throw it at him.

"Do you care that I'll be pretty enormous by then, though? I'll be eight months," I say, touching my stomach. Surprisingly, my baby bump is still barely noticeable. My mom says that's common with first pregnancies.

"Are you kidding? I didn't think you could glow any more than you already do but every day you get a little rosier and more beautiful. By the time March comes along I might have to wear a blindfold to keep from ravaging you during the ceremony."

I laugh. "I actually think a very pregnant bride fits with the whole ambience we'll have going on out there in the Redwoods. I'll be like a fertile earth fairy."

He pulls me tight against him into his arms. "Something about the way you just said fertile is making me want to drag you into the shower with me right now."

I smile and can't help but sigh as he kisses me. There's honestly nothing I'd like more.

"But Edwin is home," I whisper as my eyes flick to the closed door of his room.

"And?"

"And it would feel weird."

"We're two consenting adults, expressing our love as the universe intended. Trust me, Edwin realizes we've made love before. You're pregnant."

I smile. "Very funny. But he might hear us."

"What would you say if I told you he was quite deaf?"

I laugh. "He is not."

"Okay," he smiles, "but I'm looking forward to having our own place where we can be as loud as we want," he says as he kisses me again, "whenever we want."

"We need to figure that out soon, by the way," I say as I give him a peck in return. "Every dollar I earn for work goes toward school. And you're a student, too. How are we going to afford rent?"

"Money isn't an issue for guardians."

"What? You never told me that."

"I offered to pay your tuition and you wouldn't let me."

"Of course I wouldn't let you. It's important to me to earn my own way. But you never told me money isn't an *'issue'* for guardians. What does that even mean? You guys print your own angel cash?"

He laughs. "I didn't tell you because it isn't important."

"Okay … well, even if guardians are somehow miraculously and 'unimportantly' loaded, I have to be able to explain to my mom where our money is coming from."

"Don't worry," he says with a smile, "I have a plan that I think will make you happy."

"You, Alexander Ronin, have a plan? I find that hard to believe."

He chuckles. "You know Edwin bought this house, right?"

"Yes, of course. My mom was his realtor."

"Well, our tenant in the guest house is moving out soon. You and I could move in there if you want."

"Really?" I'm surprised and delighted. I always loved the guesthouse in the back of Alexander's yard. The main house is on a large piece of land with a little stone path along the garage that leads to the one-bedroom barn-style guesthouse far in the back. It has an open living space with a gas fireplace, a large bedroom loft, a bathroom with a claw foot tub, and a very cute efficiency kitchen. A lot of houses in San Mar have guest houses or in-law quarters. The city creates incentives to build them, due to the high demand for student housing.

"Why is Travis moving out?" I ask. Travis is a very nice grad student who I've always suspected is a guardian but I can't get Alexander or Edwin to confirm it because they refuse to reveal anyone. I've thought about just walking up to Travis and asking him—straight up—if he's a guardian angel, but I'm afraid he'll think I'm a total nutbag if he isn't.

"Just moving on," says Alexander vaguely. "He has other places he needs to go." That's as close to confirming Travis' guardian-ness as I know Alexander will ever get.

I nod.

"So are you coming into the shower with me or not?" Alexander asks.

"Not," I say with a laugh, "as much as I'm tempted."

"You're tempted?" he says with a mischievous glint in his eyes. "I think I can work with that."

I smile and my eyes trail over his tall, athletic frame, sans clothing now, and I swallow. He steps closer, closing the distance between us, and kisses me, softly at first, and then with a depth of feeling that makes me sigh, stroking his tongue with mine and causing me to melt against him.

I feel him smile as he kisses down along my neck and slides his hands under my shirt, "Shall we take this off?" he murmurs and I laugh and lift my arms and we walk towards the bathroom kissing and laughing as we peel off the rest of my clothing.

"I'm glad you changed your mind," he says as we step under the hot spray of the shower and he kisses me again.

I smile and shake my head as the water cascades over us. "You're not very angel-y, you know that, right?"

He laughs. "I love being un-angel-y with you."

I smile as we gaze into each other's eyes before he bends to kiss me softly and I slide my hands over his broad shoulders and around to his muscled back, where I pull him closer.

"You're not so angel-y either," he murmurs with a laugh as he kisses me again.

I'm sitting in the kitchen and Edwin is at the stove and I'm feeling slightly embarrassed that my hair is still a little wet, but I'm fully dressed, of course, and looking presentable and for all Edwin knows Alexander and I took separate showers. *Right?* He could believe that. At any rate, I'm trying not to think about it. I don't know why it embarrasses me, but it does. I can't help it.

Alexander is still in the bathroom shaving and brushing his teeth. I actually like it when he has a bit of a five o'clock shadow—I like the way it feels rough on my lips when we kiss and it makes him look even more dangerously attractive, if that's even possible. My knees are getting weak again just thinking about it … *"For God's sake, Jane, Focus!,"* yells my inner drill sergeant, trying to get me to come back to the present and remember where I am and what the heck I'm doing. I chuckle to myself and attempt to gather my senses.

"Edwin," I say, shaking my head to clear it, "can I ask you something?"

Edwin pours me some tea and sits down across from me in our now-familiar seats at the kitchen table. "Of course."

"Alexander once said that guardians can merge with dark guardians and then they transform into something else. Where do they go?"

He looks thoughtful. "You could think of it as disappearing into time and space."

"They just disappear? They don't leave their bodies behind?"

"Usually," Edwin says. "It's actually quite beautiful. It looks like a shooting star. But depending on the guardian's circumstances, they may leave their mortal shell behind so their loved ones aren't left with questions."

"How do their loved ones think they died?"

He takes a deep breath and meets my eyes. "Have you ever heard of dry lightning?"

"You mean lightning without rain?" In the deep recesses of my brain I vaguely remember Finn describing it once as a weather phenomenon. Like 'thunder snow,' which apparently is also a real weather phenomenon, and not the name of a superhero on the Cartoon Network for kids, despite how crazy it sounds.

He nods. "When a guardian dies in battle or if they merge and choose to leave their shell behind, the injuries are usually explained by dry lightning."

"And they don't come back if they merge?"

"No," he says.

"Not as mortals? Starting over?"

He shakes his head. "Merging is a last resort. And permanent."

"What if they did come back? Would they remember anything?"

He scrubs his chin, looking thoughtful again. "They can't … but if they somehow managed it, and it was similar to a normal transformation, I suppose their souls could retain some remnants of their experiences and wisdom," he says. "But not consciously, no, at least not at first. They'd be starting over as mortal infants."

I nod, absorbing the information. "I asked Alexander this once, but I'm not sure I understand why all the guardians don't just do that? They could merge with the dark guardians and rid the world of evil once and for all."

He shakes his head. "Evil can never be extinguished completely. Where there is light there will always be darkness. That's why maintaining the balance in our favor is so important. But to better answer your question, much like everything else in life, merging isn't guaranteed. The power it takes is immeasurable. If you attempt to merge with a dark guardian more powerful than yourself and you don't manage it, you can leave things worse off than before. It involves an enormous energy exchange … and transformation and is only to be used as a last resort. There has to be a particular type of connection between the two guardians—a willingness to take things beyond the natural order, opening yourself to risking the ultimate sacrifice."

"Does Alexander have that type of connection with Avestan?"

Edwin meets my eyes. "I'll answer it this way," he says, "Avestan has that type of connection with Alexander. His hatred and thirst for vengeance causes him to take risks. It's his power, but it's also his liability."

I swallow. "Alexander once said he would merge with Avestan if he had to." My stomach is in knots as I say the words.

Edwin doesn't respond.

"Aren't you shocked? You can't let him do that."

"Declan, if it came down to saving your life, I could never stop Alexander from doing what was needed. And now that you have the baby to protect as well, any entreaties I could make on your behalf would be even less likely to have an impact on his actions. And, to be frank with you, I wouldn't make them. Protecting your child is paramount."

"But Avestan is still recovering in Nusquam, right? How would he even know I'm pregnant? Even if he saw me right now, you can't tell. I'm barely showing."

"Avestan isn't the only one to worry about."

"You mean Alenna? You think she'll come after me again, too?"

"I was thinking of Malentus."

"But how would he know?" I ask, feeling very cold suddenly.

"None of them know yet," he says gravely, "but it's only a matter of time. Avestan will figure out, eventually, that you're pregnant and Alexander is the father. That's why Alexander and I, and the other guardians, are prepared to do whatever it takes to make sure your baby is born safe. Because a child like yours, born of a guardian and a sprite, could very well tip the balance in our favor for good."

He takes my hands across the table and meets my eyes before he continues. "We can't have any illusions about how this could go. These are grave stakes, dear. Grave stakes indeed."

Chapter Ten

Edwin's words weigh on me for the next few days as I focus on school and the life growing inside me. I thought the nausea was supposed to end after the first few months, but I'm well into my second trimester now and it still raises its ugly head on a regular basis. Like today, when I need to be at the Bing's house. It's Charlie's sixth birthday and he begged me to come to his party the last time I babysat and I promised I would. Mrs. Bing actually hired me to come, regardless, because she needs my help as a babysitter/game manager for all the kids. Any other day I would be more than happy to celebrate with Charlie, whom I love dearly, but today I keep getting overcome with these awful waves of nausea … *ugh.*

Maybe the party will distract me. I console myself with the fact that Molly won't be there. She's away at college in Santa Barbara, attending UCSB—another beautiful city on the coast where her Malibu Barbie looks must fit in perfectly. It's been refreshingly pleasant lately to go over to the Bing's to babysit, knowing she won't be there to give me the perpetual Queen B stink eye. I wonder sometimes if poor Charlie feels the same way—like time without her around is a peaceful reprieve.

When I arrive at Charlie's house there are festive balloons tied to the fence by the walkway in the front yard. Mrs. Bing must have been watching for me because she strides out purposefully to greet me and I can tell that she's already frazzled.

"Oh, Declan, thank God you're here. I should have asked you to come an hour ago. Some of the children arrived early and their parents simply dropped them off and left." She looks at me with a 'can-you-even-*believe*-these-people?' expression of incredulous exasperation before continuing. "The man who's running the laser tag game only just arrived. Thank God the kids are all set up and playing laser tag in the back yard now, I think. I'll need you to help keep them occupied and then we can serve the pizza and cake and ice cream. I have some carnival-type games, too, in case they get bored. I'll need you to run those and give out the prizes ...." Her words spill out in that brain-dump way she has of bulleting information at me, but I can see as she's talking that she's starting to slow down as she stares at me, looking me up and down in my yellow cap sleeve dress and sandals. It's a cute, casual summer dress with an empire waist that Liz got me for my birthday. I don't think it shows anything but I can tell by the expression on Mrs. Bing's face that she knows something about me is different but she can't quite put her finger on it. I haven't told her I'm pregnant since it's not overtly obvious yet. Plus, I don't want it to get back to Molly. She used to date Avestan and who knows if they're still in touch somehow. From the look in Mrs. Bing's eyes, I think she's decided that I've just put on some weight. Which, in her mind, I'm sure is a point of horror. She's wearing a fitted blue dress and she smooths her hand over her stomach self-consciously before she directs me to the side gate to enter the back yard and then conveniently vanishes, telling me she has to check on the pizza.

I push the gate open and walk toward the sound of laser blasts and hollering kids.

"Holy Schnitzel," I whisper aloud, channeling Liz with my eyes wide, as I take in the sight before me.

At least thirty six-year-olds are screaming and running haphazardly in every direction with laser tag guns and vests. The man running the game did his best setting up battle barriers, which actually appear to be simple L-shaped, rectangular frames erected with plastic PVC tubing and black felt fabric stretched across them and glued on. Numerous barriers are spread out all over the large expanse of green lawn so the kids have places to run and hide as they shoot and try not to get shot in return, but half of the barriers are already knocked down, and the other half look as if they're not long for this world. One kid must have torn off the black fabric from one of them because he's wearing it as a cape. Another kid disassembled the bare PVC frame and is now wielding the plastic tubes like swords. And another kid, dressed entirely in camouflage, is doing ninja rolls from one lonely, listing barrier to the next.

I watch as the camouflage kid holds up his laser gun in the air and yells at the top of his lungs, "Who wants to join Eagle Squadron?" Then he whips his head left and right and does another five ninja rolls to the next barrier. The problem is, he keeps getting shot in his laser vest target repeatedly as he rolls because the remaining barriers are spread too far apart. Undaunted, he just keeps rolling—over and over and over again, completely out in the open—until he finally reaches cover once more, and when he gets to the next barrier he shouts out, over the cacophony of screaming boys and laser gun blasts, "If you want to join Eagle Squadron, take cover over here!"

I can see he's getting frustrated that no one appears to be listening or reacting and he yells out again, "Eagle

Squadron! Now! Over here!" After a few more seconds with no response, his face turns tomato red and he screams out with furious annoyance, "EAGLE SQUADRON OVER HERE, YOU DIRTY DIRTBAGS!"

I'm standing with my mouth hanging open at the ferocity coming from camo-boy's six-year-old lips and that's when I finally spot Charlie. He's standing in the middle of the mayhem, laser gun in hand, and he turns and looks at the boy in camo and says, "Dude, you're taking this *way* too seriously."

I drop the present in my hand to the ground because I'm laughing so hard and that's when Charlie sees me and runs over. He almost knocks me down as he jumps into my arms for a giant hug. "Declan!" he says as I lift him up. He wraps his arms around my neck and hugs me tight as I kiss his cheek. "Hey, birthday boy," I say, "you're getting so big! And I'm so happy to see you. I brought you a present."

His eyes light up as I set him back down and crouch to his level to show him the package I dropped. It's wrapped in his favorite shade of blue with a colorful striped ribbon on top.

"Can I open it?" he asks.

I nod. "Later, when you open all your presents. I'll put it on the table with the other ones so it'll be waiting for you. I think you're going to like it." I got him a *Your First Magnet Set* he was coveting the last time we walked to the toy store downtown.

He smiles excitedly and hugs me again. "Can I ask you a question?" he asks.

"Of course."

"Are firecrackers for eating or for blowing up?"

"*What?* Why?"

"Marcus said he brought firecrackers in his pocket. And matches."

My eyes go wide. "Which one is Marcus?" I ask, trying not to panic. "We need to find him right away."

Charlie points to a group of boys near the pool running in circles and screaming. One of them is clad in only a red t-shirt and Iron Man underwear.

That can't be Marcus, he doesn't even have *pants*, let alone pockets.

Another boy, standing off to the side, is peeing into the shrubbery.

As I take it all in with stupefied horror and amazement, the good news is, my nausea has been pushed so far back on the list of urgent priorities right now that it's all but forgotten.

The bad news is, *this is going to be a very long day.*

The next few weeks of school, holidays, and finals whiz by so fast that I hardly have time to focus on anything other than day-to-day requirements and putting one foot in front of the other to get the things done that I need to. I'm slowly becoming mesmerized by the life that's growing inside me, as evidenced by my growing belly and the soft, amazing kicks that blow my mind every time I feel one. With so much else to focus on, it's been easy to forget about the danger looming ever-present in the background: dark guardians, and powerful Makers, and Avestan eventually recovering and returning to seek his hateful revenge on us once again.

I'm six months along now, entering my third trimester, and Alexander has made me feel so safe and protected all along that I find myself falling into a state of complacency.

But I know that isn't good.

I need to stay alert and keep my guard up. Avestan has had months now to recover and he could reemerge into our lives at any moment.

As the new semester starts at UCSM I'm pleasantly surprised to see that Justin and I have a class next door to each other again. Last semester we had adjacent Econ classes that let out at the same time and we got in the habit of going for coffee (or in my case, decaf herbal tea) afterwards to chat. This semester, we ended up with classes near each other in the science building.

"Wow, you're finally starting to show," Justin says as we sit down outside Campus Coffee. Similar to A-plus Coffee on the other side of campus, this café also has a large deck with a view.

"I know," I say, "it's starting to feel more real by the day."

"Are you nervous?" he asks.

"Terrified," I say with a laugh. "But Alexander and I have been going to childbirth classes, so that helps a bit. And I've been babysitting since I was twelve so I know my way around a diaper. And I love kids. I babysit this little boy named Charlie Bing who I absolutely adore. He just turned six a little while ago. His party was nuts. Do you realize what's happening at kids' parties these days?"

He laughs. "I know. I have a little stepbrother. When I was a kid my parties were ten kids in the back yard with a blow-up kiddie pool," he says. "He gets thirty kids at Jungle Jump Fantasy Land."

"I know," I laugh, "right? I'm realizing now how sedate my childhood was."

He smiles. "Hey, is Charlie Bing by any chance related to Molly Bing?"

"Yes," I say, surprised. "He's her little brother. You know Molly?"

"Wish I could answer no to that question."

I laugh. "Did you date her?"

"No, not me, thank God. She dated a friend of mine over the summer. I went over to her house with him once. I met Charlie. He's a cute kid."

"What's your friend's name?" I ask, my heart suddenly beating faster. *Please don't say Avestan.*

"Huh? Oh, it was my friend Dan. You met him once. Tall, nice guy … stupidly gullible."

My heart relaxes back to normal. I'm more on alert than I realized. "Stupidly gullible?"

He nods. "Gullible enough to believe Molly wouldn't rip his heart out and throw it back in his face. Twice."

I nod, sadly unsurprised.

I snap a photo surreptitiously of the man who I keep seeing everywhere I go on campus. He could be a fellow student who just happens to have classes in the same buildings as I do. And, I suppose, he *also* could have wandered into Campus Coffee at the same time Justin and I were there … coincidentally. But something about him is unsettling.

I tell myself the following stories, in the order of 'nothing-to-worry-about' to 'run-away-screaming-in-alarm': 1) he's a student; 2) he's a guardian who's staying extra close because danger is nearby ; and 3) he's a dark guardian here to kill me as soon as I let my guard down. Mostly likely number one is true. I know that—rationally. But that doesn't preclude numbers two or three from also being true. Only I don't think I would be feeling this uneasy if it was a guardian who was here to protect me. Then again, I *have* been on edge, regardless, and that pregnancy book warned me about surging hormones at this stage. I wonder if I'm going a little crazy?

After my last class I'm in close proximity to where Edwin teaches so I decide to go see him in his office and hopefully set my mind at ease. His door is open and I peek in to find him at his desk reading some papers. I knock softly as I step inside.

"Edwin?"

"Declan," he says, looking up with a smile, "what a nice surprise. Come have a seat. How are you feeling? The nausea still bothering you?"

I sit down in the chair next to his desk. "Better, thanks. It comes and goes but it's been gone for the last week so I hope that's the end of it."

He nods. "Glad to hear it. Now what brings you here? What can I do for you?"

"Edwin, I know you're not supposed to tell me, but I need to ask you something."

His expression shifts to a more serious one. "What is it I'm not supposed to tell you?"

"Well, there's this guy who I think has been following me all day, and I don't have a good feeling about him. I know you can't tell me who the good or bad guardians are but I need to know if my feelings are right and if this is a dark guardian. And if it is, I need you to know that he's following me. So that you can put more of the good guardians on my watch."

He smiles. "I promise you, Declan, there are always good guardians close by."

I nod. "I know, but I need to know about this one … in particular. I can't let it go."

Edwin's eyes are filled with concern. "Did he hurt you?"

"No."

"Did he try to talk to you?"

"No."

"How do you know he was following you?"

"I don't know for sure. But something about him made me feel uneasy."

"Is he outside now?" Edwin asks, turning to peer out his window. He looks in all directions.

I shake my head. "I saw him when I got out of class but he veered off when I came here. But I took a picture … without him knowing." I slide my phone out of my purse and pull up the photo.

Edwin studies the photo and as I look over his shoulder, I realize that the man looks no different than any other nondescript brown-haired man in jeans and a t-shirt on campus. Maybe I was wrong. "You felt something when he was around?" Edwin asks.

"Yes, but as I stare at the picture now it seems a bit foolish. Maybe I'm being paranoid. I'm starting to look more obviously pregnant and that has me worried because of what you said earlier. I don't want Avestan to find out." I shake my head. "I'm probably being crazy. He seems harmless now that I look at the photo. I think I'm being paranoid."

"Perhaps," Edwin says. "Or perhaps this was a dark guardian sent to find you … and his intense focus was precisely because you're starting to look pregnant."

I swallow. "So he *was* a dark guardian?"

"I don't know, Declan," he says, shaking his head, "I would need to see him in person to be sure—so I could feel his energy and see his aura. That doesn't come through in a photo. But we have to assume that perhaps Avestan has sent sentinels ahead of his return and word of your pregnancy may spread back now to those who we hope it doesn't."

The thought forms a pit in my stomach. "Edwin, I feel like I'm always looking over my shoulder. I can't live like this anymore. I need to know who the bad guys are. You need to tell me."

Edwin squeezes my hand. "I know this is hard, Declan. But trust your instincts. And remember you're never alone. There are guardians all around, all the time."

"What if Malentus comes?" I say. "I don't even know who he is. The only dark guardians I know to watch out for are Avestan and now Alenna."

"If Malentus comes, guardians will be around you, to protect you."

"That's not good enough," I insist. "I need to know what he looks like. I don't care if it's against the rules." I'm standing my ground on this one. It's not just about me anymore. It's about my baby, too.

Edwin meets my eyes. "I don't carry a photo, Declan."

"Edwin, I need *something*," I say, my eyes pleading with him. "It's killing me not knowing."

Edwin opens a drawer in his desk and pulls out a sketch pad and a pencil and turns to an empty page. *Edwin is an artist?* He sets the pad down in his lap and turns in his chair and begins to sketch. The way he has the sketch pad angled up and the way he's turned in his chair means I don't have a clear view, but I can see the top outline of a face appearing from among his pencil strokes. When he finishes, he tears out the page and hands it to me. "If you ever see this man," he says, "call me or Alexander right away."

I look at the sketch and the face that inhabits the page takes me by surprise. It's the face of a young man, early twenties, light hair, full lips, very handsome. The creeping horror I feel on seeing his likeness is twofold: one, in my mind I had pictured Malentus as far older and I realize now that I never would have recognized him, even if he'd been standing right in front of me; and two, the fact that this face—this exceptionally handsome yet ordinary face, someone I would have happily talked to in class or made chitchat with in the line at Campus Coffee—masks an evil so deep that even Edwin avoids speaking his name.

I stare at the picture for a long time and only then do I see it. Something in the eyes. Edwin managed to capture and convey with his pencil strokes something in this handsome man's eyes that, if you know to look for it, shows what he truly is, deep down inside.

This is the man who made Avestan what he is.

This is the man who left Alexander with a jagged scar running down the length of his side.

And this is the man who set the wheels in motion for Burt Fields to kill my father.

I turn back to Edwin. "Thank you," I say with uneasy conviction as I slip the sketch, hands shaking, into my notebook.

Chapter Eleven

I take the bus home and I watch for the man from campus but I don't see him again. The sketch of Malentus is burned in my mind and I scan my environment constantly for him now. I see nothing and no one suspicious the whole ride home and I'm beginning to wonder again if I was just being paranoid. Avestan is most likely still recovering, Alenna must be with him, and Malentus is probably way too busy with other evilness in his corner of the world to come looking for Alexander.

Would they really bother sending some dark guardian scout to San Mar to look in on me?

I repeat these thoughts to myself many times but, if I'm being honest, it's not a convincing argument. Alexander injured Malentus severely, striking a blow to his whole line. The knot in my stomach tells me that an attack like that won't go unpunished.

I set my backpack down on the kitchen island and open the refrigerator.

"Did I raise you in a barn?"

I turn around to see my mom, who must have just walked in, look on disapprovingly as I drink orange guava juice straight from the carton. I set it down and screw the plastic cap back on with a sheepish smile. "Sorry, mom, I was dying of thirst. I just walked from the bus stop."

She shakes her head. “It takes five seconds to pour it into a glass. But I’ll let it slide this time, only because you’re pregnant.”

I laugh. “Thanks. Do you have a date with Mark tonight?”

She smiles happily. “He’s taking me out to dinner.”

“Have you kissed the poor man yet?”

My mom blushes a little. “That’s not anything to talk about.”

“I’ll take that as a yes,” I say. By now I think Liz’s premature musings about my mother’s sex life have probably come true. I try not to think about the elaborate police officer-related scenarios that Liz has envisioned and shared with me many times as a joke. At this point I’m less traumatized than just laughing about the ridiculous images it conjures up. Liz kills me.

“Do you have homework?” my mom asks.

“When don’t I have homework?” I say with a sigh as I open my backpack and start pulling out numerous notebooks and folders and books and my laptop. I spread everything out on the counter because I like to do my homework at the island in the kitchen as my mom cooks. I can’t always—it depends on the type of assignment I’m working on because some require closed-door concentration—but I like to work here when I can. It’s peaceful being in the kitchen with my mom and I love the smells of whatever she’s cooking. I’ve been doing my homework this way since I was a kid and it feels safe … and nice. My mom has good energy. I survey the spread of books and papers lying out before me and try to decide what to tackle first.

The sound of my mom's gasp causes me to startle in my seat and look up sharply. When I see her face, my eyes follow to what she's looking at and my whole body cries out in alarm. The sketch of Malentus slipped out of my notebook when I pulled everything out of my backpack and my mom is holding it in her hand, staring at it, stricken. Her other hand is on her chest and the expression in her eyes is a mixture of both shock and confusion.

"What is it?" I ask, swallowing hard. "Have you seen that guy?"

"Yes," she says, the tone of her voice sounding bewildered. "But I don't understand … why do you have a picture of Malcolm?"

Chapter Twelve

"*Malcolm?*" I ask. "You mean the guy you dated in college to make dad jealous?"

She looks at me, still befuddled, but seemingly breaks out of her spell of distraction. "I didn't date him to make your father jealous, Declan. I dated him because he'd been after me for a while and I'd given up on your father at that point."

"This," I say, pointing to the picture with disbelief, "is Malcolm?" It's more of a statement than a question. I'm still trying to absorb what she's telling me. "The guy you dated? Are you sure?" The implications roil in my mind.

Malcolm is Malentus?

"Of course I'm sure," she says. "I'm not *that* old, Declan. I think I can remember what people look like, for goodness' sake. For a moment there I felt like I'd gone back in time." She takes a deep breath, obviously still recovering from the initial shock. "How did you get this?"

"It's just a sketch someone drew. In an art class." *Small fib.*

She shakes her head slowly as if she's trying to make sense of it. "Did they draw it from a photo? I'm sorry if I scared you. It's just that this sketch looks exactly like Malcolm did when we went to school. As if no time has passed. It's uncanny. Maybe it's his son? Do you know this person's name?"

I shake my head, still trying to comprehend whatever this means.

"Well, if you see whoever this is on campus, ask him if his last name is Valent."

Before I can answer, she chimes in again. "You know what? Scratch that. Don't ask him if you see him. Don't even mention it. Don't talk to him."

"Why?" I ask. Not because I would ever approach Malentus in a million years, but because I'm curious why she's instantly reversing herself.

"Because it ended badly," she says, "between Malcolm and me, and I'm realizing now, seeing his picture, that it just brought back some painful memories."

"What memories?" I ask warily, with a creeping feeling of alarm.

"More *feelings* than actual memories … I don't remember that time very clearly, to be honest. I hate hurting people and I stopped seeing him so abruptly when your father finally came around. I think I've tried to put it out of my mind, to be honest." She sits down on one of the bar stools. "In fact, you know what? I'm not feeling so well now. I think I'll go lay down for a minute … maybe I won't go out tonight after all."

I send a text to Alexander as soon as I've finished making sure my mom is okay. I left her lying quietly with her eyes closed and a glass of water and a bottle of ibuprofen by her bedside. I don't want her to hear me talking on the phone so I type out the words as a text and hit send.

Alexander you have
to come over

His reply comes within seconds.

What's wrong?

I tap out a quick response.

It's something about Malentus
and my mom

Within less than a second I hear a knock at the door downstairs that startles me and another text pops up.

It's me.
At the door

What? He must have traveled here by light. The fact that he was alarmed enough to do that worries me almost as much as finding out Malcolm and Malentus are one and the same. Alexander never travels by light unless we're flying together. It makes him weaker and he says it's reckless to do it in populated areas because people could see him suddenly appear and how would he explain it?

I open the door to see Alexander looking almost as stricken as my mom was when she saw the sketch of Malentus. “What is it?” he asks as he steps inside.

I motion for him to follow me through the kitchen and out the door into the garage. I close the door behind us so I can be sure my mom won’t overhear us.

“Edwin drew me a sketch and my mom saw it and she said it was Malcolm,” I say, words tumbling out.

“Wait, what happened?”

I explain the whole story to him, about my mom and dad in college, and her dating Malcolm and how it ended badly and all the way up to Edwin drawing the sketch for me today of Malentus. Alexander’s face grows grimmer by the minute but in the end he doesn’t appear shocked, which is surprising.

“Where is she now?” Alexander asks when I finish.

“Upstairs,” I say. “Lying down. She said she wasn’t feeling well after she saw the sketch.”

He nods soberly. “I understand why you asked Edwin to draw you that picture, but it wasn’t a good idea.”

“Why?”

“For one thing, because what you focus on you can draw to you.”

“Just by drawing a sketch?”

“Not just by drawing it but by looking at it, focusing on it—now you’ll be looking for Malentus everywhere. Seeking him out.”

I feel a little sick to my stomach. He's right, I did do that. *Did I do the wrong thing by insisting Edwin show me a picture?* I swallow hard. "What else?"

"What do you mean?"

"You said, 'for one thing.' Why else was it a bad idea?"

"Because of exactly what happened. Now your mum saw it."

My eyes narrow in confusion for a long beat as I absorb his words. "Did you *know* about this?" I ask, disbelieving.

He meets my eyes but doesn't answer.

"Let's go to my house to talk," he says after a wretched stretch of silence.

Chapter Thirteen

"You *knew?*" I place my fingers on my temples with utter incredulity. I can't wrap my head around what I think I'm realizing must be true. "You knew and you didn't tell me?"

"Declan, please," Alexander says, "let's go to my house to talk."

"And leave my mom here alone?" My head is spinning, I can't believe he's admitting it. *He knew? He knew about a connection to my mom and Malentus? And he didn't tell me?*

"Guardians are watching over her and the house."

"Why do we have to go someplace else?" I say, my voice rising with emotion. "Whatever you're going to tell me, you can tell me right here, right now. Otherwise you can explain to me why we need to leave just so you can spell out exactly why you would keep secrets from me."

"Declan, I want to go to my house because I can see already that you're getting, justifiably, upset about it."

"*Upset?*" I huff. "You better believe I'm upset. I'm six months pregnant and I just found out my fiancé has been keeping vital information from me about my mom and a monster!"

"Declan, please," he says, his eyes pain-filled and pleading. "Come with me. If for no other reason than the fact that what I'm about to tell you, trust me, you won't want your mum to overhear."

He lowers his voice on the latter half of the sentence and the way he says the words steals the wind from my furious sails in an instant. I look at him, unable to speak for a moment.

What could be worse than what I already found out?

"Let's go in the kitchen," Alexander says when we get to his house. "Edwin's there."

"Edwin knows, too?" The fist of betrayal in my stomach clenches tighter.

When we enter the kitchen Edwin has his back turned and he's stirring a cup of tea. "We have to tell Declan about her father," Alexander states firmly as he walks in. "Right now. No more delaying. It's time." The sound of the metal spoon swirling against the sides of the ceramic cup stops abruptly.

"You mean about my mom," I say.

"No," Edwin says grimly as he turns around and looks at Alexander, "he means about your father."

I glance at Alexander questioningly.

"We'd better sit down," Edwin says, gesturing to the kitchen table. "Can I get you anything first?"

My stomach is in knots and I feel faint. I just want them to spit it out. "No, just tell me. Please. Whatever it is."

Alexander pulls out a chair for me and we all sit down in our usual spots with Alexander next to me and Edwin across the table.

"Mrs. Jane saw the sketch you drew," Alexander says to Edwin. "She recognized Malentus as Malcolm, a man she dated briefly in college."

Edwin nods, silent for a long minute as he stares down at his hands on the table in front of him. "That would make sense."

"That's what I thought, too," Alexander says.

"How does that make sense?" I ask as I watch their faces with equal parts horror, fear and mounting anger. "How does any of this make any sense at all?"

Alexander turns to me in his chair and takes my hands in his. "Declan, I'm sorry about the way you're finding this out."

"Finding what out?" My stomach sinks with dread.

"There's a reason you're a sprite," Alexander says quietly. "It's because your father was a guardian."

I blink, unsure I heard him correctly. "My father was a *guardian?*" I turn to look at Edwin. Surely he can't believe this, too. "But how can that be?"

"He fell in love with your mum, like I did with you," Alexander says. "He wanted to be with her."

I think back to my mom's story about my dad resisting at first, insisting they could only be friends. "But I thought it never happened before?" My mind is racing, trying to piece together disparate information into some form, anything, that makes sense.

"Guardians don't speak of it," Edwin interjects, "because of what happened."

"But why? *How?*" I ask. "And why wouldn't you tell me my dad was a guardian? That's a good thing. Right? So why wouldn't you tell me?"

Edwin and Alexander look at each other but don't answer.

"No," I say, shaking my head determinedly. "This can't be true. You said if a guardian fell in love and kissed a mortal they would be a fallen guardian and have to start over. And the mortal would die."

I look from one to the other but they still don't answer. "My mom is *clearly* still alive," I say with a disbelieving harrumph, "and my dad didn't start over. He was my dad for ten years! Until he was killed because of Malentus."

"Your dad became a mortal," Alexander says quietly.

"*What?*" I look from Alexander to Edwin and back again waiting for them to tell me that this is all a bad joke, but neither one of them answer. "How is that even possible?"

"He struck a deal," Edwin says, "with Malentus."

"What?" The word emerges from my throat as barely a whisper because all the air has been punched from my lungs. *My dad made a deal? With a dark angel?*

My eyes flick from Alexander to Edwin and back again as the implications sink in. "Are you saying he was a *fallen* guardian?" My heart freefalls through my center as I say the words. Now I understand why Alexander didn't want to tell me.

"Yes," Alexander says, "but he did it to save your mum's life."

"He gave all his power to Malentus, in exchange for becoming a mortal," Edwin explains. "He didn't join the dark guardians."

"But isn't that just as bad?" I ask. "Giving all his power to the other side?"

Edwin glances over at Alexander.

"Malentus had your mother trapped in Nusquam. Your father struck the deal to save her." I can see the anguish in Alexander's eyes as he continues. "Having been in a similar situation, I can imagine struggling with that decision myself."

Edwin looks at him sharply. "It was not a good decision," he says.

Alexander returns his look with pointed disapproval.

"But we understand the forces at work that caused him to make the decision he did," Edwin adds, relenting somewhat.

I think back to my mom's story and her confusion about the time with Malentus. "Does my mom know all this?"

Edwin shakes his head. "I'm sure one of the conditions was that she not remember. Has she said anything?"

"She said her memories of Malcolm and how it all ended are fuzzy. She said she wanted to put it behind her. She started feeling sick when she saw the sketch … maybe on some level she was remembering."

"If her memory of Nusquam was erased, that would make sense. The feelings, but not the clear memories may have come back to her," Edwin says.

I nod, feeling ill myself. The memories I have of being in Nusquam and the hopelessness and the despair—filling me like thick, black, choking smoke—still haunt me in my sleep.

"If Malentus was dating your mother, it would explain how he got her to agree to go with him," Edwin says, "willingly."

I'm barely listening anymore. Memories of my dad rush over me. How my mom said he 'sparkled' the first time she ever saw him. How she said he looked like hell when he came to her finally and kissed her for the first time. *Because he'd just given all his power away and become a mortal?* How happy they were together, and so in love …. Other memories flood back, too, with new layers of meaning attached: how my dad always used to tell me people to avoid when I was little. How he told me I was special and that my anxiety was actually my superpower and someday I'd learn how to use it. '*What you think of as a weakness is actually your greatest strength.*' At the time I thought it was the hokum of positive parenting that all moms and dads tell their kids to make them feel better. *Did he know I was a sprite?*

"How am I a sprite if my dad became a mortal, though?" I ask. "He wasn't a guardian anymore when he became my dad."

"Your father must have retained some remnants," Edwin says. "You can clip a guardian's wings, but they'll still find a way to soar. It may be why Malentus targeted your father later, by influencing Burt Fields. Or perhaps Malentus couldn't abide your father's happiness in spite of giving up all his power—"

"Or it could have just been a matter of a dark guardian skirting his end of the deal," adds Alexander with disdain, "as they always do."

"So this is the second connection Avestan was talking about?" I ask.

Alexander nods. "We think so."

"It may also be the reason Avestan came to San Mar and targeted you so quickly," Edwin says. "Malentus may have suspected that you were a sprite and sent him to find out."

I turn to Alexander. "And you weren't going to tell me any of this?"

"Declan," he says, his eyes filled with tortured regret, "I didn't want to cause you anymore pain. Especially not after you just found out your father was murdered—I saw how much it hurt you."

"I asked Alexander to wait," Edwin says.

I look at them both. "You knew all along?"

"No," Alexander says, his eyes insistent. "I never lied to you. I didn't know about the connection when you asked me about it before."

"How long have you known then?" I ask.

"Not long," Alexander says.

"How long?" I repeat firmly.

"About a month," Alexander says quietly as he meets my eyes.

I release the breath I was holding in. "You've known for a *month*? Since before winter break?"

"I didn't want to bring it up over the holidays," Alexander says. He looks pained, sick even.

I stand up and take a step back from the table. "You both told me you would tell me if you found out anything. And yet you've known for a *month*? And neither of you said a word?"

"Declan, I—"

"I don't want to hear anymore," I say, cutting Alexander off. "I trusted you … and you didn't trust me enough to tell me the truth …." I look in his eyes, trying to convey the pain I feel, but when Alexander starts to stand I hold out my hand rigidly between us. "I need to be away from you for a while," I say with hurt and disbelief permeating every molecule of my body. "I don't know for how long. Maybe forever. I never thought I'd say this, but you betrayed me, Alexander. You betrayed my trust."

Alexander stands up but doesn't move from the table. He looks torn, stricken. Edwin watches me turn to leave with deep sorrow in his eyes.

"Don't follow me," I say over my shoulder with anger and sadness as I walk out the front door and slam it behind me, utterly heartsick.

Chapter Fourteen

I start to grasp the enormity of what I just learned when I get home and sink down into the couch. My dad was a guardian. A *fallen* guardian. He fell in love with my mom and struck a deal with the devil, basically, to save her. And save himself. He made sure he got something out of the deal, too—the chance to be a mortal with my mom.

Can I blame him?

If he had to give up his power, why shouldn't he get something in return? And he only gave up his power to the dark side when his back was against the wall and he had no other choice. I remember the helplessness I felt when I saw Charlie suffering terribly in Nusquam. I would have done anything to save him. I imagine my dad must have felt the same way. He had to save my mom. And if he had to make a tortured decision, why not try to squeeze out as much of a happy outcome as possible? So he and my mom could at least be together, as mortals?

The fact that I'm trying so hard to twist my thoughts into a pretzel to rationalize what my dad did tells me that something doesn't feel quite right.

I worshipped my dad. Envisioning him now in a less than one hundred percent positive light is disconcerting. It feels like a betrayal. My dad was a good man. He spent his life helping people at the law office with their cases. He did a lot of pro bono work, and he volunteered in the community.

He loved my mom and he did what he had to do to save her. How can that be bad?

The fact that he struck a deal with Malentus to be able to do it, and he gave his power to the dark side in the process, is something I can't wrap my head around right now. Because I'm also feeling knocked off my axis from another betrayal: Alexander knew all this for over a *month*. And how much longer would he have kept it from me? If fate hadn't intervened and my mom hadn't seen the sketch that Edwin drew? Was he going to wait until after I had the baby? Or maybe never?

Where is my mom? The thought hits me like a brick suddenly and I feel a strong need to run upstairs and check on her. When I get to her room I breathe a heaving sigh of relief when I see her still lying on her bed with her eyes closed.

"Mom?" I say softly.

Her eyes flutter open. "Hi, honey," she says, trying but failing to execute more than half a smile.

"Are you okay?"

"Yes, just tired mostly. But don't worry, I'm sure I'll be fine."

"Can I bring you anything? Are you still going out with Mark tonight?"

"No, I called him and told him I'm not feeling well. He offered to come over and bring me some soup but I told him I just need some rest."

I nod.

"I'm fine, honey," she adds, "but thanks for checking in on me."

"Oh, okay, I should let you sleep then," I say, but I hesitate before closing the door.

"Is there something on your mind, hon?" she asks.

I don't answer.

She pats the empty side of the bed beside her. "Come over here and sit with your mom for a minute. I don't have to sleep just yet. I'm just resting. Talk to me."

I swallow the lump in my throat and walk over to sit down on the bed next to her. There are so many things I want to tell her. So many things I want to ask her. It's a very lonely feeling being with Alexander at times because I can't ask for advice or talk about my worries in a normal way with the people I love. I can't fully confide in Liz or Finn or my mom, and that means a big part of my life—an important part—is basically off limits to conversation. It's a blessing and a curse, being with a guardian, because it means I can only hash things over with myself. And, unfortunately, endless rumination within the confines of my own brain isn't the best way to gain perspective. Not to mention the fact that it can be maddening.

If only my mom knew … *maybe she does?* Could my dad have told her the truth at some point during all the years they were together? Alexander once said that by revealing the guardians' existence to me, he put me in added danger and that's why he resisted. My heart tells me that my dad probably kept it to himself for that same reason … *but what if he didn't?* The idea that my mom has been holding her secrets while I've been holding mine—each of us convinced that we could never reveal them to each other—would certainly be ironic, to say the least. I push aside my hurt and sadness over everything I learned tonight for a moment and decide to probe, tentatively.

"What is it, sweetie?" my mom asks, reaching over to stroke my forehead and smooth my hair out of my eyes. "You look so sad."

I shake my head. I don't know what to say.

"Are you worried about me?" she asks. "Because I'm telling you I'll be fine, honey. I don't know what came over me. Probably a 24-hour thing. But nothing for you to worry about, I promise. As you know, the Jane's are a hardy lot." She smiles and reaches over to squeeze my hand.

I smile back. True to form, my mom is both endlessly optimistic and worried about others more than herself. "Alexander and I had an argument," I say.

She nods, quiet. "Was it over something big?"

"No," I say, but my eyes get misty. I don't want to admit it's a big deal because she already witnessed two of our breakups over the past year and I don't want her to think we're breaking up yet again. *Although won't we have to? How can I be with someone I don't trust?*

She pats my hand. "Couples argue. It's *how* you argue, and how you make up, that matters."

"What do you mean?"

"I mean if you argue respectfully. If you approach an argument trying to see the other person's perspective. If you both truly listen and take the time to understand each other's side. That's what matters. I read once that a show of contempt for your partner is a death knell for a marriage. If you love each other and you approach every argument truly looking for a solution, you'll find one. The trick is to start with the belief that the other person is well intentioned—it makes it easier to listen when you'd rather slam the door in their stupid face."

I choke out a laugh of surprise as tears spill over and my mom laughs with me and helps me wipe them away.

"Did you argue with dad a lot?" I ask.

She shakes her head. "Not about anything important. And trust me when I say that 99 percent of what feels important isn't. At least not when you gain a little time and perspective. *'People of good will can always find common ground,'* your father used to say. They used to call him the 'wonder mediator' at work because he was always able to get two parties with intractable differences to finally come together and find some space to agree. And somehow he and I always agreed in the end, too. Because we approached arguments with the same objective: to find a solution that worked for both of us so that we could move on to the business of spending the rest of our lives together, happily, which was always our ultimate goal."

I smile. She makes it sound so easy. *But what if the other person lied to you? Or at least kept something important from you.* "I think I just need some time to myself," I say quietly, "to mull things over for a while."

"I should mention that apologizing is important, too," she adds. "On both sides. Your father also used to say that people who refuse to ever admit they're wrong or say they're sorry have the most to be sorry for." She pauses for a moment before continuing. "He always got a sad look in his eyes when he said that … I sometimes felt that he had a great sorrow in his past that he wanted to apologize for. Something he didn't want to talk about."

Wow. Maybe she understood him better than he realized. I feel like this could be a possible opening for me to find out what I want to know. "Did you ever think dad was an angel?" I ask. I don't know how else to broach it other than to just blurt it out.

"Of course he was an angel," she says with a soft smile. "He was an angel from the day we met. My angel."

I watch her expression carefully. "But did he ever seem like *more* than that?"

She looks at me with confused humor in her eyes. "What do you mean?"

"Did he ever tell you anything? Like a story of how he came to be?"

Her brow furrows with amusement. "How he *came to be*? I think he came to be just like the rest of us, sweetie. But if you mean his background, certainly, he told me how his parents died before we met, which was very sad, and where he came from, in Wisconsin."

I search her eyes for any signs of covering or obfuscation. "So you never thought he was an angel," I say, trying one last time. I watch her carefully as I say the word *angel* but all I witness is confusion.

"You mean like a *real* angel? With wings?" she asks. "I think he's an angel now, sweetie, if that's what you're asking. In fact, I know he is. A man as kind and decent as your dad would continue to do good things in the afterlife. I know that in my heart."

I nod. "You mean as a guardian angel," I say slowly. Once again I watch her eyes as I emphasize the word *guardian*. Nothing.

She smiles. "Yes, I'm sure he's watching over all of us. But what's with all these questions, honey? Is it because I told you your dad spoke to me?"

I shake my head. "No, I just was asking," I say. "The older I get, the more I wish I could have known dad as an adult, not just as a kid. So I could have understood him more. And asked him about things."

My mom squeezes my hand and her eyes well up. "Me, too," she says. "You were the light of his life, you know. He used to go on those long walks with you and he'd come back so happy and glowing inside. He told me once he never enjoyed talking with someone, and also being blissfully silent with someone, as much as he did with me and his little girl. He felt like you understood him. Even at that young age."

I meet her eyes and mine well up, too. "Thanks, mom," I say as I give her a hug. "I really miss those walks."

She cradles my face in her hands and kisses me on the forehead. "I love you so much, sweetie," she says. "Your dad would be so proud of the woman you grew up to be. Please know that."

I nod silently as tears spill over once more and we continue to hug with my head on her chest. "I'll let you rest now," I say finally when I draw back and she gives me one last kiss on the cheek.

I go into my room and lie down on my bed, staring at the ceiling. I think for a long while about my dad, and about life, and about Alexander, and about the decisions he made, and the decisions my father made, and the decisions I've made, too.

And I think about the fact that my emotions are a jumble—a Gordian knot—and I have no idea how to feel about everything I've learned and what I'm going to do.

Alexander once said that trust is the most important thing. You can love someone deeply but if you don't *trust* each other, implicitly, a relationship is never going to work.

How can I trust Alexander when he chose not to tell me something so important? After he promised me he would?

Something even a dark guardian like Avestan was willing to tell me?

Chapter Fifteen

This is depressing. I'm six and a half months pregnant and the future I had planned, and that of my baby, is uncertain. For two weeks now, I've been putting Alexander off, telling him I'm not ready to talk yet at length … telling him I'm still thinking. And I *have* been thinking … a lot. About how much I love Alexander and how happy I feel when I'm around him, and the way we "spark" together. And about how much we both love this baby I'm carrying inside me.

I've even done contortionist somersaults in my mind to fully inhabit his perspective and understand why he didn't tell me: It was the holidays. It was bad news. It was bad news about my dad, in particular, which would be especially heart-wrenching to me, especially coming on the heels of me finding out my father was murdered only a few months before. And it was bad news not only about my dad, and not only while I was pregnant, but it connected me and my family, again, to Avestan and Malentus. To evil. I saw the torment in Alexander's eyes when he told me. I hear it in his voice, still, every time we talk. I know he regrets it and I know why he tore himself up inside making the decision he did.

I know all these things and yet my mind still always settles on the matter of *trust*. In retrospect, I can see that there were times perhaps over the break that something was on his mind, but in those moments I had no idea. We continued on with our blissful lives together, unimpeded, full steam ahead, with him harboring a secret and me none the wiser.

That's what doesn't sit right with me, and it's what I'm having a hard time getting past: that he could look me in the eye all those times and not say anything.

"Are you and Alexander still in a funk?" asks Liz as we sit sipping our teas at A-plus Coffee.

"I just can't get over the fact that he kept a secret from me," I say.

"Are you ever going to tell me what this mysterious secret is?" Liz asks. "You're starting to make me wonder if he's in the witness protection program or something. Or maybe he's a fugitive? Do we have an extradition treaty with Australia?"

I push her arm. "He's not a fugitive."

"Made you smile," she says. "First time in weeks."

"I'm fine. I just need more time to think this through I guess."

"Well it's not like you're going to cancel the wedding."

I don't answer.

"It's *that* serious?" she says.

"I don't know, Liz. I don't think so. I just need more time. To think."

She puts her hand over mine and looks at me with worried eyes. "You don't have to do anything you don't want to, you know. I have no idea what's going on with you and Alexander to make you feel this way, but one thing I *do* know is that he would never abandon you and the baby, no matter what you decide. Alexander's one of the good ones. Believe me, I can spot bullshit from twenty paces, and somehow that guy got model looks *and* a heart of gold."

I meet her eyes and nod softly. Of course she's right.

"But don't ever tell him I said that," she adds. "I have to maintain my reputation as a hardass."

I let out a small laugh. "Sorry to break it to you, but he knows about your hard candy shell and soft center," I say, and she smiles. 'But you're right. I don't have any worries about him not taking care of me and the baby."

"Good. And remember, Finn and I can help, too. And your mom. We'll all pitch in. I'm looking forward to being an auntie. The coolest auntie on the planet."

I smile.

"The point is," she says, "you're not alone. That little guy or girl in there is going to be born into a world with a team of people who already love him. Or her. And *you've* got us, too. We're all here to catch you, if you need it."

I squeeze her hand. "You'd better stop now or I'm going to start crying," I say, my eyes welling up. "It's the pregnancy hormones."

"Yeah, right," she says. "As if you haven't had a marshmallow heart your whole life through. But if you want to blame your misty eyes on pregnancy hormones during this nine-month stretch, I'll play along."

I laugh.

"Made you smile again," she says.

I take a deep breath, feeling better. "Can we talk about something else other than me for a while? How did you do on that chemistry exam you were worried about?"

Liz fills me in and just like that we're off and running on a thousand other topics—from school to Finn to nutty customers at Jack's Burger Shack that make us laugh until we cry. Liz has, once again, like the true friend she is, diverted my mind from my troubles.

And it's in that moment, when I'm relaxed and feeling happy again and at my most vulnerable, that I'm shaken back to reality.

The fear of what I've been facing all along is suddenly in front of me and it's so jarring my whole body goes numb. Across the large expanse of grass beside the deck stands a man, watching me. I can't say I would have even noticed him in the crowd, and perhaps that's what's most disturbing. But the one thing that made me notice—the thing that's making every ounce of my blood pool at my feet—is that the man's face is the face in the sketch Edwin drew. And those eyes, the eyes that Edwin captured so unnervingly, are even more dark and piercing than they were on the page. I can feel it, even from a distance.

"Can we go?" I say suddenly to Liz, standing up. My heart is racing and I feel faint.

"Why?" she asks, "I thought your next class didn't start until two."

"I have some work I want to get done first, in the library." I look over to where Malentus was watching me but now, thankfully (and also very disturbingly), he's gone.

Did I imagine it?

"Okay, I'll walk over with you," Liz says, as she stands up with me.

I grab my backpack and turn around to leave and that's when my knees buckle and I wobble and nearly fall to the floor. Liz reaches over to hold me steady as I grab the seatback of the chair I was sitting in for support.

What she doesn't understand—what she couldn't possibly understand—is that I'm finding it hard to breathe because Malentus is standing directly in front of me.

"I couldn't help noticing you're pregnant," he says, his voice dark and smooth with an undercurrent of threat as he reaches out his hand to touch my stomach. "How many months along are you?"

Chapter Sixteen

"Wow," Liz says when we leave the coffee shop. "Talk about stranger danger, that guy had some serious balls. First of all, touching your stomach—you don't touch someone's freaking stomach, or, for that matter, *any* part of their body, without asking them first. And second of all, my mom always says unless you see a woman actually crowning in front of you, you should never, *ever* say anything about her being pregnant unless she brings it up first. I learned that the hard way when I asked my mom's friend Margery when she was due and it turned out she'd had the baby six months earlier. How the hell was I supposed to know? But that woman has hated me ever since." She shakes her head. "There's no going back on a comment like that … absolutely no way to recover."

I nod, not answering. I'm happy to let Liz fill the silence as we walk to the library because I'm still too shaken to speak.

"Are you okay?" she asks. "Don't worry about that creeper. Maybe he's one of those freaky weirdos who hits on pregnant women. He probably wanted to know how far along you are so he could make sure you fit his fetish profile."

I shake my head. I was struggling to think and wasn't really listening to Liz's chatter too closely but I can't help but react when she says the words *fetish profile*. I cough out a surprised laugh.

"Oh thank God, I was starting to get worried," she says when she sees my hint of a smile.

"*Fetish profile*? Is that even a thing?"

"Of course it's a thing," she laughs. "Are you familiar with the contraption known as the internet? Spend a day exploring the weird things that auto-complete on Google and you'll want to scrub your eyes out with bleach."

I shake my head again with a smile.

"Listen, don't worry about that guy. After the talking to I gave him, I doubt he'll come within a thousand feet of either one of us ever again."

Liz doesn't realize it, but that's one of the things that has me even more worried. I was frozen when Malentus spoke to me and put his hand on my stomach, and I couldn't stop Liz from telling him how rude he was and to leave us alone. The girl has zero fear and she had no idea who she was messing with.

"It's fine," I say, as we reach the campus library. I can't act too freaked out or Liz will worry about me. "I'm okay. And please don't bother ever talking to that guy again if you see him. People are going to say things now that I'm starting to show. And I've heard some of the women complain in my childbirth class about strangers touching their stomachs. I need to get used to it and be prepared to step back."

"You sure you're okay?" she asks, meeting my eyes. "You were acting kinda funny."

I nod. "I'm just gonna go inside to do some homework before class," I say as I gesture to the glass doors at the library in front of us. "You don't have to walk me in."

"All right," she says, pulling her phone out of her backpack and looking at the screen. "Finn just texted me anyway. He needs a ride."

"I wish he would go ahead and take that driving test," I say.

She nods. "Seeing Zeno get hurt hit him hard. He said he never wants to drive now."

"I know," I say, "and I understand … it was awful … and scary." I think back to Zeno lying in the street, whimpering and suffering, and Avestan staring smugly from the corner. "But I still think he should take the test. For his own sense of self-determination. He was ready. And to not drive because of such a sad day … I just want him to get past it. I've been talking with him about it a little. I hope he comes around."

She nods. "I honestly don't care if he ever drives, though, and I've told him so. Pretty soon the whole concept of human drivers will be obsolete anyway. Once the singularity happens and the evil robotic overlords take over with their driverless cars, they'll steer all of us trusting humans straight into the ocean. Did you hear about that tourist last week who followed her maps program and drove straight off the pier?" She laughs. "It's already happening! Anyway, I've gotta go. Call me later."

I nod and can't help but laugh back as we hug goodbye, but when I turn to go into the library my expression quickly changes. I walk directly through to the café inside on the first floor and keep going, out to the deck in the back. When I get there I find a deserted corner and pull out my cell phone to call Alexander.

"You're sure it was Malentus?" Alexander asks. He came to the library to meet me and we're sitting in a quiet corner of the deck, outside.

"Yes."

"And he knows for sure that you're pregnant?" he asks.

"I don't know, Alexander," I say with exasperation, "I assume so since I'm starting to look like I'm hiding a soccer ball under my shirt and he asked me how many months I am."

He takes my hands and meets my eyes. "Hey, it's okay. I've got this. I have a plan."

I stare back at him with anxious worry weighing heavily on my shoulders, but all the worry in the world can't hold back the trace of a smile that appears at the corners of my mouth. "You always have a plan."

"Yes," he says, returning my smirk. "I do. For a reason. I knew something like this was only a matter of time."

I swallow. "What are you going to do?"

"Keep you safe. Whatever it takes."

"That's a pretty vague answer," I say. "But maybe it's because it involves more secrets that you conveniently won't tell me." My voice is laced with heavy sarcasm.

"No," he says quietly, looking wounded. "Never again."

Immediately I feel a stab of pain in my heart at the look on his face and I remember what my mom said about arguing respectfully and assuming good intentions on the other person's part. "I shouldn't have said that."

"No, I deserved it," he says. "Declan, I'm sorry for not telling you about your father right away. I know I've been telling you for weeks now how sorry I am but I want you to understand that I realize I made the wrong decision. And I'll never make a mistake like that again."

I meet his eyes. "I'm trying to understand," I say, "but I'm having a hard time with the trust part. When I think back to the times we had together over the month that you knew and you didn't say anything … I mean, we had some pretty intimate conversations and you never said a word."

I can see the pain in his eyes when he answers. "You're right."

When he doesn't say any more, my heart softens. In our previous conversations he always added *why* he did what he did—that he made the choice because he felt it was the right one at the time, even though it tore him up inside. His many explanations helped me understand where he was coming from, but they also left me feeling like he was defending himself and not really understanding how betrayed I feel. Now, his simple admission: "*You're right,*" is finally left to stand alone, surrounded by silence, and my heart takes one step closer to his.

"So what are you going to do?" I ask. "About Malentus."

"First priority is keeping you and the baby safe," he says. "If Malentus is here, Avestan and Alenna may be as well. We'll send out the word to everyone to stay on alert. If I could, I'd take you away from here until the baby is born."

"I can't do that," I say, shaking my head firmly. "I have to finish school. And I won't leave my mom … and Liz and Finn."

"I know," he says, taking my hands, "that's why I said *if I could*. I knew you wouldn't go for that option. And that's why it's not a part of my plan. I would never take you away from all the people you love."

I stare into his soulful green eyes and feel that deep connection between us, stirring. "You're one of the people I love, too, you know," I say softly.

Surprise flickers over his face and it makes my heart hurt again as I realize that he must have questioned if I still love him. "I'm glad to hear you say that," he says, his voice gruff and restrained.

"But I'm not ready to say we're back together. I'm sorry."

"I understand," he says quietly and I can feel the pain in his heart because it's in my heart, too, and I feel a tug on the string of light between us, connecting our hearts together.

"I'll wait as long as it takes," he says as he looks into my eyes. He holds my gaze, for an endless stretch, and I feel that spark that has always drawn us together. I feel our molecules, vibrating in harmony, and I want to touch him. I want him to hold me and kiss me and tell me everything's going to be okay. I want to wrap myself in the safety of his arms and never let go. And I want to use whatever power I have to protect him, too. But something inside me isn't ready to forgive—not yet—so I don't. And I fear I'm worse off because of it, with more permanent scar tissue on my heart.

Instead, I keep my heart cordoned off a little, and I make plans to meet with Alexander and Edwin tomorrow to discuss what they're going to do. Maybe it's because I'm not forgiving enough or wise enough to see the forest for the trees, or maybe I'm just not ready to talk, or to listen—to anything—including whatever the next plan is. But right now, all I can say is, I feel like I'm in survival mode. I have to go to class and then I have to go to work and then I have to do homework, go to bed, and wake up tomorrow and do virtually the same thing all over again. I have to keep putting one foot in front of the other. I don't have time to stop and indulge my worries about dark guardians and even-more-evil dark guardians who stalk and threaten me at school. Because it's not just me inhabiting this body anymore, it's my baby, too, and I can't give in. I can't devolve into a quivering, anxious mess.

I find the light in my core and take a deep breath. I have to trust that I can protect myself and that Alexander will also protect me, fiercely, as he always has. And I do—I trust Alexander with my safety and that of my loved ones more than anyone else in the world.

And that's when I realize I haven't really lost my trust in Alexander. It's still there, as strong as ever.

It's just temporarily buried—under anger and disappointment, but mostly sadness.

Chapter Seventeen

"How are you doing?" Justin asks as we sit at Campus Coffee chatting. I'm pulling apart a blueberry muffin and drinking hot herbal tea and he has a cappuccino in front of him. It's been cold, rainy, and overcast all day today so we're sitting inside.

"Okay," I say, "a little tired."

"Yeah, that's common in the third trimester."

I look at him, amused. "And you know this because …?"

"My stepmom. When she had my little brother."

"That's right, I forgot you've been through all this before."

"Yeah, my little brother's a pain in the ass. But he's kinda cool, too," he says with a smile of genuine affection. "How's the wedding planning coming along?"

"Well, considering there almost wasn't going to *be* a wedding, I guess it's coming along fine now. Still on track."

"Wait … *what?* What happened?"

"Nothing," I say, "there was a problem but I think it's resolved now." I realize as I say the words that I'm starting to sound like Finn with his 'resolved versus unresolved/pending' ledger he keeps in his head.

"Did Alexander back out?" His words are delivered with a fierceness that touches my heart.

"No, nothing like that."

"Then what was it?"

"It was me. I was having a hard time dealing with some … *obstacles.*"

He meets my eyes. "Obstacles big enough to call it off?" he asks.

"I wasn't sure."

Justin sets down his drink and stares at me for a long time. His eyes are expressive, changing from uncertain to determined and back again, many times. "Declan," he says finally, "I need to tell you something."

"What is it?" The anxiety in his expression has me worried.

He hesitates before answering and then he takes a deep breath in and begins to speak. "I'm sure it's no secret how I feel about you," he says, meeting my eyes. "Or maybe you don't realize it, maybe it *is* a secret—"

"Justin, I—"

"Please just let me say this. I need you to know something," he says, his eyes pleading and earnest. "When I first saw you, I thought you were cute. *More* than cute—I'm not gonna lie. That's why I tried to get us assigned together, at first. Then we became friends and I liked you even more. Knowing I would see you is probably the only thing that kept me at that brainless job at Fields and Morris, scanning like a drone. Well … *that* and the fact that I pay my own tuition and really had no choice."

I smile and he grins back, his smile reaching his deep blue eyes.

"But I knew you had a boyfriend," he continues. "And then when you broke up with him and I kissed you I thought I had a chance."

He looks down for a moment and then back up, meeting my eyes. "You set me straight, unfortunately. But you said you wanted to remain friends, which surprised me. And you meant it, which surprised me even more … because that meant you enjoyed our friendship, maybe as much as I do … because I really do, and the way I feel, I don't know … I just think about you ... all the time …. *Shit,* I'm rambling now, aren't I?"

I can't help but smile. "Justin, I—"

"Please, I've gone this far and I need to finish." He looks up into my eyes. "*Please.* I want to say this."

I remain quiet and he takes a deep breath and continues. "I accepted that you were with Alexander, and I accepted that all you and I will ever be is friends. I accepted it and I can live with it. But if there's any chance …" He looks up and meets my eyes. "What I need you to know is this: Declan, if those obstacles you mentioned, whatever they are, become too great and you don't go through with the wedding, I want you to know that you don't have to feel like you're all alone." He swallows. "Because I've been in love with you for a while now, and I would be there for you … and we could raise the baby together … if you wanted."

My eyes well up and threaten to spill over because I'm so touched by Justin's sincerity. I can see it in his eyes and I can literally feel it between us, in his heart. And I'd be lying if I didn't acknowledge the fact that, if it wasn't for

Alexander, I'd be hard pressed not to see Justin as more than a friend. He's smart, and cute, and funny, and kind … and a part of me craves the simplicity of his proposal. If I wasn't with Alexander perhaps the dark guardians would leave me alone? I know it's unrealistic but I indulge myself with the fantasy of Malentus and Avestan assuming the baby is Justin's. Just a normal baby that they won't take notice of or try to harm. I allow myself to imagine a normal life, with a mortal. Someone I could talk about with my friends and my mom, with no secrets to hide. Someone who will grow old with me, and who my baby could watch grow older, too, and come to know as a father figure over time. With Alexander will there always be danger? I know for certain that he brings complications and things to work around. How will I explain to my mother, or to our child, that he never ages? Not to mention our friends. A normal life, for a split second, is seductively refreshing and attractive in its mundane simplicity.

But only for a second.

Because the idea of a life without Alexander is unimaginable. The way he makes me feel when we're together, and his honesty and kindness, are all things I could never turn away from. Sitting here now, hearing Justin profess his love to me has paradoxically only solidified my love for Alexander. I feel my heart swelling within my chest at the clarity of this realization. I can't wait to find Alexander, to tell him I forgive him, and to "move on to the business of living the rest of our lives together, happily," as my mom said. That's been my objective all along—I was just distracted by all the other emotions swirling inside me and I lost track and forgot for a time.

All these thoughts race through my mind in mere seconds, but I realize Justin is still sitting before me, searching my eyes and waiting for an answer.

I reach out to touch his hand across the table. "Justin, you have no idea how much it means to me that you would say that. And offer that. And trust me enough to lay your heart and your cards on the table in that way."

"But …" he says, sensing my answer.

"You're right, there is a 'but.' I'm sorry, I really am, but I'm in love with Alexander," I say. "We have some obstacles but we'll get through them, and I'm going to marry him. I'm having his baby."

He nods with acceptance and a tinge of sadness in his eyes. "That's what I thought, but I knew I'd regret it forever if I didn't let you know how I feel."

I smile softly, my eyes threatening to overflow again. "I'm glad you did. I *appreciate* that you did. I don't know if it's the pregnancy hormones or what, but I feel an appreciation for the people I care about and who care about me on a whole other level lately. It's like *deep*," I say with a laugh as I wipe away an errant tear that manages to escape.

He smiles.

"And what you said truly touched my heart," I add.

I can feel him searching my eyes when he replies. "If I ask you a question will give you me an honest answer?"

"Of course."

"If Alexander wasn't in the picture, would you have accepted my proposal?"

"If Alexander wasn't in the picture there wouldn't have been a proposal because I wouldn't be pregnant, and I wouldn't be getting married."

"You know what I mean," he says. "If Alexander didn't exist, would you have gone out with me? As a boyfriend? Are you attracted to me in that way?"

I consider how to answer. I don't want to give him false hope but I promised to be honest. "Yes," I say, meeting his eyes.

"That's not a pity answer?" he asks.

"Do you honestly think I would give you a pity answer?"

He smiles. "No. What was it you said about how I tried to kiss you? I 'came at you like a thief in the night?' No one mean enough to say that would be nice enough to give me a pity answer."

I laugh. "I don't know if I should take that as an insult or a compliment."

"Definitely an insult. I figure if I insult you now we can go back to being friends again."

"Well you miscalculated wildly on that one."

He laughs. "Can I ask you another question?"

"Yes."

"Does Alexander have any flaws?"

"What do you mean?"

"It's just that he's a really nice guy and he seems so perfect. Please tell me there's something wrong with him. Like he's a terrible dancer … or he has raging gingivitis."

"Everyone has flaws," I laugh, "but no, no gingivitis and I'm the one who's the terrible dancer."

He smiles. "Figures."

What I don't say, what I *can't* say is that yes, Alexander does have a flaw, a big one, if you can call it that.

He's a guardian: an amazing, wondrous thing that also brings unrelenting danger in the form of Avestan and Malentus. The "flaw" is that dark guardians are chasing after him, and chasing after me, and after our baby, and they're never, ever going to stop. Not until they destroy us all.

Unless Alexander can somehow make them stop ....

But he already bears the scars of his previous tries.

Chapter Eighteen

"You were right," Edwin says gravely as Alexander and I sit with him at their kitchen table, once again, to discuss guardian business. "Malentus is here."

I nod. "When I saw his eyes, I knew. Avestan's eyes are black and cold but nothing like the way I felt when I looked into Malentus's eyes."

"He wasn't trying to shield his energy," Edwin says. "He wanted you to know who he was."

"It felt like he was toying with me, like prey. The same way I always feel when Avestan shows up and scares me like that."

Alexander nods. "They relish it. Feeling your fear and dread makes it more satisfying to them."

"Please tell me your plan isn't to go after Malentus again," I say.

"It isn't," Alexander says, "for now."

"We can't risk engaging with them before the baby is born," says Edwin. "Until then we've called in reinforcements for protection. It will be every guardian's duty to ensure your baby is born safe and healthy. They know what the stakes are."

"Do you really think this baby is going to change the world?" I ask, placing my palm over my stomach protectively.

"I dismissed stories before," Edwin says. "And any scientist will tell you there's no harm in planning for a feasible, potential cataclysm, but the opposite can't be said. We have to assume this could bring on the final battle between dark and light, and possibly tip the scales in our favor—for eternity. We have to be ready."

I swallow and glance over at Alexander. "What will you do after the baby is born, then?"

"We'll end this once and for all," Alexander answers. "I know Malentus's weakness now and I've always known Avestan's. But first things first. We can't be distracted from anything other than protecting you now."

"But won't our baby still be in danger, even after it's born?"

"Your child will always be protected," Edwin says, "but if the prophecy is true, once he or she is born, the stage is set and the energy unleashed will be unstoppable."

"All because of our baby?" I ask, instinctively touching my stomach again.

Alexander nods. "Did you expect anything less than the most powerful baby in the universe from the two of us?" He smiles and it's the first joke he's made in weeks, and I can feel the hesitancy behind it, as if he's unsure if we're back on joking terms yet. It makes my heart hurt a little to sense him testing the waters.

Edwin stands up. "I have a meeting with some other guardians so I'll leave you two. Any more questions for me before I go?" he asks.

"Not for now," I say, looking up at him. "Thanks, Edwin. I appreciate you always looking out for me."

He smiles. "That's what we do."

After Edwin leaves I turn to Alexander. "Can we talk?" I ask.

"Of course," he says, looking surprised. Up until now I've been avoiding him for the most part, other than to call him about Malentus yesterday when I was so frightened.

"Can we go in your room?" I ask.

Instead of answering he stands up and holds out his hand for me. I take it and we walk hand-in-hand to his bedroom. When we get there he pauses in the doorway and I can tell he's waiting to see where I sit. When I choose the bed, he follows and sits next to me. I turn to face him and he does the same.

"Alexander," I say, taking a deep breath, "I understand why you did what you did. And over these weeks, as I've had time to think about it, I can't tease apart what portion of my reaction was a feeling of betrayal versus what fraction was shock and sadness over the truth about my dad. It's been a lot to absorb over a short time—first that my dad was murdered and now that he may have inadvertently set that in motion for himself by making a deal with Malentus in the first place. I still haven't processed it all."

Alexander nods and meets my eyes, silent. I see worry in his expression and that makes me press forward. "But the point is," I say, "I love you. And I want to be with you. Always. And that hasn't changed. I was angry but I choose to get over it and trust you so that we can move forward, together. I know you're sincere and I know you won't keep the truth from me again. I feel like I can see your heart, and feel it, and I know that's true. I only hope I haven't damaged what we have by some of the things I said and by making you wait so long." My voice cracks on the last few words and I look up and meet his eyes with hopeful worry.

"Declan," he says, taking my hands, "you could never damage what we have." The look of compassion and love in his eyes goes straight to my heart. "And I would wait for you forever."

My eyes get misty as he searches my expression. "I'm sorry about how I handled things," he continues. "I'm still working out how to be a guardian to someone I have such intense, protective feelings for, and I made a mistake."

I nod.

"Does this mean you still want to marry me?" he asks.

"Yes," I smile. "More than ever."

His answering smile warms me like the sun. "I love you," he says as he pulls me into his arms and kisses me softly. I sigh at the familiar feeling—*oh how I missed this*. "I forgot how good you taste," he groans as he kisses me again, tenderly.

"It's my lip gloss," I murmur back with a laugh, "it's flavored."

He smiles. "No, it's you," he says, "all you."

I wrap my arms around him, basking in the feel of his body against mine. "Make love to me," I whisper and he smiles and kisses me again, harder this time. "I've been holding this in for weeks," he groans, deep in his throat, as he trails his mouth along my jaw and down along my neck. I smile as I remember how good this feels, to be with Alexander and to be kissed by him, all over. Gradually he makes his way back to my mouth and kisses me again, softer this time. And as I revel in the taste of Alexander's lips, which I denied myself for far too long, he deepens the kiss once more, reminding me how we were made for each other. I slip off his shirt, gliding my hands over the hard plane of his chest, and drink in the sight and scent of him. We take turns removing each other's clothing, slowly, as we explore each other's bodies anew and lie down. "You sure this won't hurt the baby?" he murmurs into my ear as he kisses me and pulls me against him until my back is cradled against his front like nesting spoons. He caresses my breasts and kisses my neck and as his hands glide over me I turn my head to kiss his lips. "Yes," I breathe, "the doctor said it's fine." I can feel his smile as he presses against me. And then, as we've done so many times before, we make love.

And just like the first time, the feeling is too intense and delicious and exquisitely sublime for words.

Chapter Nineteen

"I have an idea for the baby's name," I say as I lie in Alexander's arms. I forgot how good his warm skin feels against mine as we cuddle in a languorous daze, indulging in our usual pillow talk.

Alexander reaches down and caresses my baby bump. "He says he likes Alexander Jr."

I laugh. "That's a possibility, but hear me out."

"Did he just kick?" Alexander asks with amazement. His palm is still resting on my stomach.

I reach down to rest my own hand there and the baby kicks again. "He must feel your energy," I say. "He's showing you he likes it as much as I do."

He moves his hand and the baby kicks once more and Alexander smiles. "There's no miracle like the miracle of a baby," he says with a level of awe in his voice I don't hear him convey very often.

"That's exactly the name I had."

"What is?"

"Miracle," I say. "And we call her Mira for short. Or Michael if it's a boy, which sounds a little like miracle."

I can see that he's thinking for a moment. "I like it," he says after a short delay. "I thought it might be hard to agree on names, but our baby literally will be a miracle: the miracle baby of a guardian and a sprite. It's perfect."

"You really like it?"

"Yes, I really do."

I raise my head up to kiss him. "I love you."

He smiles and takes a deep breath. "You have no idea how good it feels every time I hear you say that again. I almost forgot how this feels—between us. At the risk of sounding corny, whenever I hear that song, *Powerful*, it makes me think of how it feels, being with you."

"The one with Ellie Goulding?"

He laughs. "Yes. It seems inadequate to compare it to a song, but the way we are together—it's so good. And intense."

I smile up at him. "It's not corny. And I feel it, too. I missed this—being with you. Being in your arms. And feeling this way."

He rakes his fingers through his hair. "I've been a miserable wretch these past few weeks without you."

I plant another kiss on his lips and his clouded expression turns to a smile. "Well then it's good that that's over," I say, not wanting to dwell on it a moment longer. "Can I ask you something?"

"Anything."

"What are we going to do as the baby gets older?"

"What do you mean?"

"I mean how are we going to explain to our child that their father never ages? Not to mention my mom, and our friends, and every other mortal person in the world who doesn't realize they're walking amongst guardians all day long?"

"We'll deal with that when the time comes."

"How do guardians usually deal with it? With being around mortals and never aging?"

"We don't stay in one place for too long, so it's not a problem."

"But we can't do that."

"I know," he says. "We'll sort it out when the time comes. Don't worry."

"You say that, but what does it mean? *How* will we sort it out? Move away? Because I don't want to leave everyone behind."

"I don't know yet, but we'll find a way."

"But what will you do? Dye your hair gray or wear a mask or something?" I ask with a laugh. "Will you get a degree in Hollywood makeup?"

He smiles. "Don't worry, it'll be sorted," he repeats. "But first we need to focus on getting married and having our baby. I think we're getting ahead of ourselves."

"This from the man who always has a plan?"

"I promise you, I'll have a plan when the time comes." He meets my eyes but I can see a shade of worry *(or is it something else?)* in them. "I won't let anything get in the way of our life together."

"For the record," I say, "I've made peace with the idea that I'm going to get old and wrinkly and you're going to stay looking like an Australian supermodel. I just don't know how we're going to explain it to the rest of the world, that's all."

He laughs. "We'll find a way," he says again and then he kisses me, for a long time, until I forget what we were even talking about.

Chapter Twenty

It's only two weeks before the wedding, which is nearly eight months into my pregnancy, and *yowza*, my stomach has really popped. I'm sitting on Finn's couch with my feet up on a large ottoman as I pet Zeno lying beside me. Willow, my cat, was resting on my lap earlier for about three hours while I was doing my homework before I came over here, and I think Zeno must smell Willow's scent on me because he looks especially content as he snoozes in and out, snoring softly. Willow and Zeno used to play a lot when they were younger but Zeno doesn't go outside as much anymore and I've been keeping Willow inside as often as she's willing, ever since Avestan caused that girl to hit Zeno with her car. I've often wondered about that girl ... she seemed stricken and genuinely upset. But could she have been a dark guardian who did it on purpose? Or was she an unlucky pawn in Avestan's evil games? The madness of trying to figure everyone out all the time and slot them into categories: good and bad; angel and mortal, can spin your head in circles if you don't shut it down somehow. I try to make assumptions and move on, accepting the fact that I'll never know for sure. Otherwise, I'll drive myself crazy.

My last shift at Jack's Burger Shack was yesterday and now, for the next four months, I'll be enjoying the extra time on my hands. Of course, once the baby's born I know all my time will be filled, but until then it feels oddly strange and freeing to only have to focus on school and not have a job to go to. I've also been volunteering every

Tuesday at the homeless shelter, but I talked with Sarah, the director, and she encouraged me to take the same four months off from volunteering as well, to focus on the baby. She gave me a cute little baby onesie as a gift and when I opened the present and saw it I wondered, not for the first time, if Sarah could be a guardian. On the front it says "Mommy and Daddy's Little Angel" in script lettering. Whether by design or coincidence, it made me smile.

On my last day at Jack's, Jack took me aside and gave me an envelope. He joked that the secret recipe for a Hula Burger was inside it but when I opened the flap and saw what it was, I burst into tears. He paid me, in one lump sum, my average weekly salary for all the weeks I'll be taking time off. He called it a combination baby and wedding present from him and Al. He said Jack's Burger Shack was doing well, partly due to my friendly face behind the register, and I deserved it. He also instructed me to tell Liz that it was a reward for always remembering to wear my Jack's Burger Shack t-shirt to work. I laughed and hugged him for longer than he probably wanted me to and I got his shoulder wet from my tears. I blamed it all on pregnancy hormones.

"Man, you're big," Finn says as he plops down on the couch next to me with Zeno between us.

"Thanks a lot, Finn."

"I just mean you're slim here," he says, gesturing up and down with his hands to my upper half, "and you're still tiny here," he says, now gesturing the same way to my lower half, "but here," he says, making the gesture of a rounded sphere around my belly, "you're very large."

I laugh. "It's called a baby."

"I realize that. It's just that you look normal, except for this giant bump."

I shake my head. "I *am* normal. And I still get around like normal. I have this thing called a belly band that I wear when I go running now—although I don't really run, it's more like walking fast at this point. Anyway, it supports the uterus."

"I don't want to hear about any feminine products," Finn says.

"It's not a feminine product," I say, "it's a workout thingie for pregnant women. Jesus, I can't even think of the right words anymore. All my brain cell power is going to the baby."

"That doesn't seem wise from an evolutionary standpoint."

"It's not like I have *control* over it, Finn," I say with exasperation. "And I'm exaggerating anyway. How could I be speaking to you right now if all my brain cells were gone?"

"You said it, not me," he says with a shrug. "I'm not supposed to argue with you after the seven month marker."

His comment snaps me out of my mild crankiness. "What? Why?"

"That's what the book recommends."

"What book?"

"The pregnancy book."

"You read a pregnancy book?"

"The top five pregnancy books, according to sales and average review ratings."

"Are you kidding? Why?"

"I wanted to make sure I knew what to do if something happened while we were together."

"You mean like if I went into labor?"

"That's one scenario."

"But wouldn't you just take me to the hospital?"

"Cars can break down or there could be traffic. A surprising percentage of babies are born on the way to the hospital."

"So you were reading up on how to deliver my baby for me on the side of the road?" I ask, incredulous.

"Among other things."

"Is that one of the scenarios on your list of things to worry about that you have alphabetized in your brain?"

"It is now," he says with a furrow in his brow.

I reach over and squeeze his hand. "Finn," I say, "thank you … for caring about me that much. But I can assure you that I'll make it to the hospital in time. Please don't add that to your worries."

"Statistically, especially with a first pregnancy, it's unlikely. I'm not worried."

"Okay," I say with a smile, "you're not worried."

"The scenarios to be more worried about are pre-term labor, preeclampsia, placenta previa, pla—"

"Stop," I say, holding up my hand. "Please. I know all the things to be worried about. I read the books, too. I don't want to hear about it though. It's like bad juju."

"That's not a thing."

I smile. "I thought you weren't supposed to argue with me."

"I forgot."

"Have you thought any more about taking the driving test?" I ask, changing the subject.

"I took it."

"*What?*" My mouth is hanging open. "When?"

"Three weeks ago."

I realize, in my gobsmacked state, that he probably didn't tell me for a reason. "Did you pass?" I ask tentatively.

"Yes."

"What? You *did?* So you have your license? Oh my God! Congratulations, Finn, this is a big deal! How did you do on the test? Was it hard?"

"The DMV test administrator said I was her first perfect score," he answers with a proud smile.

"Oh my God, that's amazing! Why didn't you tell me?"

He shrugs. "It never came up."

I shake my head in astonishment. "What do you mean it never came up?! Finn, we need to celebrate. What made you change your mind about finally taking the test?"

"I wanted to be able to drive you to the hospital if you went into labor."

His words hit me with unexpected emotion and when I meet his eyes, tears pool in mine. "You did it for *me?*"

He looks down and pets Zeno cuddled between us on the couch. "When I saw that girl hit Zeno with her car, I froze. Zeno ran out in front of her and she didn't have time to react. It wasn't her fault. I decided I didn't want to ever be behind the wheel of a 4,000 pound vehicle that could hurt an animal, or a person, without warning like that. But now that I've had more time to think about it and review the statistics again, I realize that I can be safe and minimize the risks. I don't want to be helpless if you or someone else needs me. And, ultimately, the same reasons that motivated me to ask you to teach me to drive in the first place still exist. I want to have the option to drive myself places I need to go."

He glances up at me and I nod.

"That being said," he continues, "I still mostly ride my bike. It's good exercise and much safer statistically. Bike fatalities are typically less than two percent of motor vehicle fatalities each year. Of course bike trips make up just one percent of trips in the U.S., so it's hard to parse the numbers unless you know how many miles all the cyclists are covering or take into account what time of day it is and how experienced the cyclists are, but, by most calculations, it's still statistically safer. And I'm very experienced so the risk goes down even further for me …"

I reach over and touch his forearm so he'll look up at me again. His earnest, touching sincerity combined with practicality squeezes my heart. I stand up and walk over to give him a giant bear hug. "I'm glad you did it," I say.

"Thanks for teaching me," he says, hugging me back, "so patiently. Like Mrs. Denuzio."

I laugh. If Mrs. Denuzio can somehow see us right now from wherever she is, I hope she knows I paid it forward, using her as a model. I pull back and sit down beside Finn and I reach over and squeeze his hand. "You know, you don't have to worry about me and this baby, Finn. I want you to know that. Please don't add me to your list of worries. There are a lot of other people around to help, too. I trust you with my life, but please know it's not all on you."

He nods. "I know."

"You're going to be the greatest uncle," I say and I mean it—kids adore Finn. He gets down to their level and plays with them and he understands and appreciates their curiosity about everything. He joined me once at the park when I was babysitting, and Charlie still talks about it to this day. The last time I babysat he asked me when Finn was coming to play again.

I look up and meet Finn's eyes. "That's all you need to focus on, just being a super fun uncle … and my friend, like always. *Truly.*"

"I don't need to focus on being your friend. We just always have been."

I smile. He's right. From the moment we met in pre-K all those years ago and I sensed his goodness, I hoped he'd be my friend. It always feels good to be with Finn, surrounded by his steadfastness and pure honesty. "Do you want to go out to lunch and celebrate getting your license?" I ask. "My treat. Does Liz know?"

"I don't think so."

"You don't *think* so?"

"I don't remember telling her."

I shake my head. He has the entire California vehicle code memorized but he doesn't remember if he told his girlfriend he can drive. "We're calling her," I say, "and she's meeting us out. Where do you want to go?"

"I thought I was supposed to help you study for your physics exam?" he asks.

"We can study after."

"Let's study first. I'm not hungry yet."

I shrug and reach for my backpack on the floor to pull out my physics textbook. "Okay," I say, "apparently I can't argue with you since I'm past the seven month marker."

He laughs and I open the book between us so we can get to work.

Two hours later, both of us now firmly in the hungry column, Finn calls Liz while I walk to the large, front picture window in his living room to pull aside the curtains and look outside to see if the sun has come out yet. My shoulders slump when I see that it's still cloudy and overcast. As I let the curtains fall back into place something catches my eye. I push the curtains aside again and I immediately feel faint and grab the window frame for support.

There, on the same corner that Avestan stood when Zeno was lying in the street, stands Alenna, watching me with an intensity that makes my legs feel as if they're buckling beneath me.

I quickly let the curtain fall closed and step to the side, away from the window.

But almost immediately I stop and think *what am I doing? Hiding like this?* I step back to the window and pull the curtain open again and stare at Alenna with as much intensity as she's directing at me. I can feel her energy, even from this far away, and my insides are quivering with fear, but I stand strong and give it right back, as best I can. I refuse to let her know I'm afraid. After a few minutes she turns and walks away and I breathe a heaving sigh of relief.

I can't help feeling that it's just as Alexander and Edwin predicted.

The dark guardians are closing in, before the baby is born.

Chapter Twenty-One

"I'm more worried than before," I say as I lie in Alexander's arms in his room. My head is on his bare chest and the steady metronome of his heartbeat plays in my ear as I trace the contours of his ab muscles with my fingers.

"I know," he says as he strokes my hair and bends to kiss the top of my head. "But I won't let anything happen to you. Or our baby."

"Is Avestan in San Mar now, too?" I ask, lifting my head to meet his eyes.

"No one's seen him yet." He slides down, resting his elbow on the bed and his head in his hand, until we're on our sides, face to face. "It's going to be okay," he says, looking straight into my eyes. He glides his hand along the contours of my hip and then slides it forward to caress my very large baby bump. "Everyone is focused on protecting this baby, most of all me." He leans down and kisses my stomach, his lips soft and warm on my skin.

I nod. I keep bringing it up and I know I need to let it go. Worrying never solved anything. I've been extra cautious and Alexander has been practically at my side every minute. The other guardians are also doing all they can. I need to trust that there's nothing else to be done for now and focus on school and our fast-approaching wedding and the imminent arrival of our baby.

I also need to remind myself that I'm not helpless. I have power, too. Even if I feel like cowering in a closet most days.

"Are you still attracted to me?" I ask. "Like this?" I look down at my large belly between us as we lay on our sides.

"Do you really question that after the fun we just had, not an hour ago?"

I smile. "Was that making love or hot sex?"

"First time making love," he laughs, "second time the latter. Would you agree?"

"Yes," I say, still smiling from ear to ear.

"Declan," he says, looking into my eyes, "you're more beautiful to me every day that we're together. And the fact that you're carrying our baby inside you only makes you more so. I'd ravage you 24/7 if I wasn't worried about tiring you out or hurting the baby."

I smile and push his arm. "It doesn't hurt the baby. And I'm not tired."

"In that case, come here," he says with a laugh, pulling me close for a kiss.

"Wow," I say, "this isn't like you."

"I strongly beg to differ."

"No," I laugh, "I mean it isn't like you to not have a plan, building up to a big occasion like our wedding night."

"I do have a plan: to make love with you as often as possible."

I push his arm. "I mean a plan like holding off for a while, leading up to our wedding night. You know, the whole anticipation thing."

"Is that what you want?"

"Truthfully?" I say, "No. Don't get me wrong, I appreciate the way you elevate anticipation to an art form—it's like, *masterful,* really."

He laughs.

"But right now," I continue, "when I'm feeling so big and I hardly recognize my body sometimes, it makes me feel good that you still desire me so much. In that way. Not to mention the fact that I enjoy making love with you."

"As do I," he says with a smile, "as you well know." He leans over and kisses me softly and his expression shifts to gentle sincerity. "I considered suggesting we hold off for a while leading up to our wedding, but the simple truth is, I love you. And I want you. And I desire you. All the time. Expressing it in this way is the most natural thing in the world, and what you and I have is so rare, and extraordinary." He pauses and cups my cheek in his hand, holding my gaze. "Declan, I want to talk with you, kiss you, make love to you, and be with you as much as we can. I want to make the most of every minute we have together, and I want to etch these days and all these moments leading up to our wedding and the birth of our baby in my mind for eternity."

My eyes get teary as I lean over to kiss his lips. "Me, too," I say softly. "I couldn't love you more."

He kisses me back and pulls me into his arms. "Are you ready to feel intensely good again?" he murmurs as he kisses along my neck.

I laugh. "Are you?"

He smiles. "Always," he murmurs as he kisses me again. "Let me show you how much I love you and how good you always make me feel."

And then he shows me, slowly, one more time, how much he means it, in every sense.

Much later, as we drift off to sleep, I think back on what Alexander said, playing his words over and over in my mind, making me smile: *I want to make the most of every minute we have together ... I want to etch these moments leading up to our wedding and the birth of our baby in my mind for eternity.*

But something prickles at the edges of my thoughts, leading to a sudden shift in my interpretation as I slide into sleep.

Is he savoring our time now because of what he plans to do after the baby is born?

Chapter Twenty-Two

"I can't believe it's only two days until your upcoming nuptials," Liz says as we sit in our usual spot on the deck at A-plus Coffee.

"Upcoming *nuptials?*"

"I'm tired of saying wedding all the time, thought I'd change it up," she says. "Too weird?"

"Not so much weird as formal, like you're an old English aunt in a nineteenth century novel."

"That makes me like it more."

I smile. "Call it whatever you like as long as you're there. Your parents are still coming, too, right?"

"We're coming together with Finn and his parents—the Warners and the Coopers, one big crazy clan," she says dryly. "By the way, I should warn you that my mom is giving you a wedding present. I have no idea what it is but it's in a frighteningly ginormous box. The good news is, Finn and I got you something normal that will hopefully counteract whatever craziness you find when you unwrap that thing."

I laugh. "Is it wrong that I'm seriously intrigued and looking forward to opening it?"

"More misguided than wrong."

"I hope it fits in our new place, whatever it is."

"Again, seriously misguided," she says. "When do you move into the guesthouse?"

"On our wedding night. Alexander's been getting it ready. I haven't even been inside since Travis moved out. Alexander says he's fixing it up for us. But he's just getting the basics in place. We're going to decorate it together after we move in."

"I already talked with him about holding the baby shower there," she says with a nod. "But I don't understand why you wanted me to wait until after the wedding to throw you a shower. And why no wedding shower? You're kind of being a party poop, I have to say."

I laugh. "Our wedding is so small, it just seemed silly. And I thought I'd be more relaxed afterwards for the baby shower. Plus, it'll be closer to the baby's due date."

She raises her eyebrows. "You're cutting it a little closer, sister."

"Edwin already bought us a crib and all the essentials," I say. "Alexander has that all set up, just in case. The baby shower can be for all the fun stuff like tiny little baby clothes and baby blankets and other adorable baby stuff I can't think of right now because I have pregnancy brain."

She smiles. "I guess I'll tell Finn to take back all those boring cases of diapers he bought for you at Costco."

"*No,*" I wail with a laugh, "I'll need those."

"Well how are we supposed to get you adorable little baby clothes if we don't know what the sex of the baby is yet?" she asks. "And do you realize I'm dying of curiosity? You're killing me here."

I smile. "My profuse apologies for killing you by not finding out the sex of my baby, so I can be surprised. Think of it as payback for all those sex jokes about my mom and Chief Stephens."

She laughs. "All I'm saying is, I'd be waaay too curious to wait until the end. But I reluctantly respect your ridiculously impractical restraint," she says, reaching over to give me a fist bump.

"Very funny."

"And you're still not planning on going on a honeymoon?" she asks.

"We can't," I say, "not now, anyway. Not with school. And it's not like I can travel anywhere far in my condition, anyway. But over the summer we plan to go to Australia." I can't tell her that we'll be flying by light to anywhere we want. Alexander and I put together a list of places we want to go together.

"Good, because without a honeymoon, what's the point of getting married?" she says. "By the way, I predict that soon after your wedding there'll be another one."

"*What?*" My heart leaps in my chest. "You and Finn are getting married?"

She laughs. "Good God, no. I told Finn I don't think I ever want to get married and he says he's fine with that. He told me that getting married forces some people to stay together longer than they should and every day that we stay together, without being married, is a day that we chose each other, and that means more to him than a government-issued certificate that's difficult and costly to undo."

I smile. "That's both shockingly cynical and also very sweet."

"He has a way of doing that," she says. "As you know. And I actually agree with him. Not that I'm knocking marriage for other people, like you and Alexander. That's just me being me."

I smile. "Well, someday Finn's probably going to ask you," I say. "It's orderly—it's in his nature."

"And I'll answer when and if that happens. But I told him I don't want to get married until I'm settled in my career. Not before thirty at least."

"I thought you just said you told him you don't want to get married at all?"

"I've told him a few things …" she says, "it changes. It'll probably take him ten years to put together a mental spreadsheet to analyze all the factors to consider before marriage anyway."

I laugh. "Well if you're not the ones who are getting married then who are you predicting a wedding for?"

"Who do you think? The object of all my good jokes: your mom and Chief Stephens."

"*What?* What makes you say that?"

"You're moving out of the house … the chief of police probably moves in—'for protection' they'll say—and before you know it, *bam* … a tasteful wedding at a winery or something. You know how it works with old people."

I laugh. "You know what? I actually hope you're right, but I don't think my mom is anywhere near ready for that big of a step. I don't even know if she's slept with him yet."

Liz places both of her hands on my shoulders. "Oh my God, you sad little naïve girl," she says slowly, shaking her head. "Yes, I know it's hard to accept, but your mom is having sex. With a man. Possibly right now. And it could involve handcuffs."

I laugh so hard I spit out my tea. "Stop it," I say. "You're killing me. I don't want that in my mind. And by the way, that is so far out of character for both of them, it's crazy."

"I know. Exactly. That's what makes it so funny."

I smile and shake my head. "The last time you said they were having sex they weren't, so I think I can read what's going on a little better than you on this."

She raises an eyebrow, accepting my challenge. "Well I hate to burn another image into your hard drive but the other day when I rapped on your door looking for you, your mom answered, in the middle of the day, looking quite disheveled yet paradoxically happy. Oh, and Chief Stephens' squad car was in the driveway. Now I don't know how *you* read those facts, but I read them as a little *Afternoon Delight*. And I'm not talking about the song from the seventies that my mother used to play incessantly."

We're both laughing now, hard.

"You're under arrest, Judy Jane," Liz says in her best deep-voiced impersonation of Chief Stephens, "for being too sexy under the law."

I can't stop laughing.

"… and I can assure you that's not a nightsti—"

"Stop," I plead, holding up my hand and holding onto my stomach at the same time, as we fall into another round of paroxysms. "You're going to make me go into labor." Picturing Chief Stephens saying those ridiculous things to my mom … and Liz's voice impersonation … it's all too much. I think I'm going to pee my pants.

Each time our laughter dies down we look into each other's eyes and start giggling all over again. Finally, somehow, we manage to calm for good and we're left smiling in the afterglow.

"God, that was funny," Liz says, taking a deep, cleansing breath. "Something about picturing your mom slays me … good ol' Judy Jane." She chuckles again and we both smile and sigh together, still catching our breath.

"I hate to be a buzzkill after all that," she says, "but I need to tell you something. Do you remember that creepy guy who came into Jack's a long time ago and told me to tell you hello? The one who used to go out with Molly Bing? And who you told me later was mean to Charlie?"

Any remaining laughter dies in my chest. "Yes," I say as horrible dread washes over me at what she's going to say next.

"You told me if he ever came by again to let you know, so I'm letting you know. He didn't say anything bad or anything like that, but he came into Jack's and said to tell you congratulations on the wedding."

"You talked to him?" I can't hide the alarm in my voice—not only at the fact that Avestan was here in San Mar, but that he approached Liz again.

"I had to. He walked up and ordered a hamburger. What was I supposed to do?"

"Did he say anything else?"

"No, Jack came to the front and told me he'd finish taking his order because it was time for my break. Creepy guy changed his mind and left."

I nod, dazed.

"But oh yeah," she says, "I forgot, I guess he did say one other thing … but it seemed harmless. He also said to tell you he has a present. For you and the baby."

Chapter Twenty-Three

I sit, still dazed, after Liz had to leave to go to class. There's no point in calling Alexander. I have a class in ten minutes and afterwards I'm meeting him at his house. I can fill him in then on the news that Avestan is here, for sure now, and he's delivering threats through Liz.

I walk to class and manage to sit through a long lecture and discussion afterwards without retaining virtually anything. I look down at my notebook when class ends and see that I've been taking notes all along. Thank God the note-taking portion of my brain can apparently work on autopilot while the rest of my brain stews endlessly over comments made by dark angels.

When I reach the parking lot where I parked my mom's car, it's quiet. I haven't been riding my bike to school since my stomach got bigger because it was getting harder to balance and I was worried about crashing and hurting the baby. Justin was right about my butt becoming granite over time from biking all the hills at school, though, and I like the shape I'm in because of all that conditioning early on. Over the last few months I've mostly shifted to walking everywhere because it feels good and I like the exercise, but Alexander has insisted I either get a ride or take his or my mom's car for this last stretch of time leading up to our wedding and the birth of the baby. Just to be safe. I'm glad he did because I'm tired and looking forward to getting home quickly. It's dinnertime and the sun is preparing to set.

I press the button on my key to unlock the car and as I get close enough to open the door my heart sinks because the front, driver-side tire is completely flat. *Crap.* I slide my backpack off my shoulder and, as I turn back to swing it up on the hood so I can pull out my phone, I gasp aloud. Malentus is standing in front of me with his hand resting casually on the roof of the car.

"Would you like some assistance?" he asks. His voice is smooth, like a curl of black smoke that wraps itself around you, looking for a way inside.

"Assistance with the tire that you probably flattened yourself?" I say, trying to hide my mounting fear with anger.

"Enough pressure, applied correctly from all sides, can produce desired results," he says, his eyes dark and self-satisfied.

I peer to my left and right uneasily. *Where is everyone?*

"Declan," he says, "I know you may find this hard to believe, but I don't want to hurt you. I'm here to help you." The way he speaks slowly, with precise articulation, reminds me of where I've heard this before.

"Yes, I remember Avestan telling me something similar," I say dryly, "right before he trapped me in Nusquam and tried to kill me." I'm weighing my options on what to do next: *Run? Try to extract my phone from my backpack quickly and call Alexander?* When I see my history professor walk into the far end of the parking lot I feel monumentally safer and I take a deep breath.

"How's this," Malentus says, "I'll fix your tire for you. All I ask is that you listen to the truth first, about us."

"I know all I want to know about dark guardians," I say as I watch my history professor stop where she stands. She makes brief eye contact with me and then pulls out her phone to make a call.

"No, I mean *us*. You and me. And our connection. There's a reason I sent Avestan to find you when you turned eighteen."

"And I suppose you came here to tell me."

"Yes, I came here to give you the truth," he says, his voice seductively smooth. "I don't know what the guardians have told you, but they have a nasty habit of withholding essential information."

"Excuse me, can you tell me what time it is?" The voice startles me and I turn to see a man standing by his car a few spaces down. I didn't even see him walk up.

"It's half six," Malentus says with irritation, answering him. The man nods and looks at both of us and gets into his car. *Was that a guardian? Then why is he leaving?*

For some reason I feel emboldened and I turn back to Malentus with anger rising within me and I feel the warmth in my core—my light stirring—as I speak. "I don't need to hear whatever you have to say. I already know about your so-called 'connection' to my family. You forced my dad to make an awful deal with you, and then, when you saw that he managed to make a happy life for himself in spite of it all, you couldn't resist coming back and manipulating your evil puppet strings until he was killed in the end anyway. You sent Avestan to find me because you were worried my dad passed along his power, despite the fact that you stole that away from him. Did I miss anything?"

Malentus looks taken aback. “It’s difficult to steal something,” he says with smooth smugness, “when it’s offered freely.”

“Freely? Or under duress?” I say. “You were torturing my mom in front of him.”

“I was *dating* your mom in front of him.”

I’m sickened by his answer. “I’m not surprised that’s what you’d call it.”

He shakes his head. “Is that what your so-called guardians told you? The guardians whom you trust so implicitly? You asked me if you missed anything and I’m compelled to inform you that, yes, you did miss something. The most important piece of the puzzle, in fact.”

“I’m not interested in anything you have to say,” I spit out with disgust. “And you know what? I don’t even need my car. I’ll take the bus.” I grab my backpack and begin to turn in the direction of the bus stop and my history professor, who I can see is still talking on her phone.

“I’m your father, Declan,” Malentus states matter-of-factly.

The words fall over me like a heavy shroud and I stop moving, stunned.

“They kept that part from you, I take it.” His voice is dark and smug.

I turn back to face him. “You’re lying,” I say, bile rising in my throat.

“The man you call your father raised you, but you come from me.”

"You're *lying,*" I say again, anger swelling in my chest. "You're scared of me and you're scared of the child growing inside me and you'll say anything to serve your purposes and get me to listen to you."

"Do I look scared to you, Declan?" His voice is sickeningly smooth.

I stand firm, but inside I'm shaking. "My father was a good man," I insist, "and you're pure evil."

"And yet I'm your father," he says with a ring of finality. "So what does that make you? And what does that make that child you're carrying?"

"This is a trick," I spit out. "You want to harm my baby."

"Why would I want to harm my grandchild? A grandchild who holds my power? The question is, how do *you* feel about your child? Now that you know the truth?" His words drip acid. "Maybe I should be protecting the baby from you? And the so-called guardians?"

"You're a liar," I say with disgust, and desperation. *Could any of this be true?* "And you're sheer evil. I can see it in your face. Your eyes are dead, and dark, and bottomless. When I look in the mirror I see my dad's eyes staring back at me. I know who my real father is."

He nods, slowly. "That's what Frank hoped, Declan—that his influence, along with your mother's, would overcome your lineage. And perhaps it did. On the surface. But deep inside you, parts of me are lurking and someday you'll realize that good and bad and right and wrong are relative terms. Perhaps your child will understand that from the start." He leans closer, meeting my eyes with his cold, dead stare before continuing. “What I hope, as your father, is that you’ll let me protect your child from the guardians you mistakenly think are looking out for your best interests,” he says darkly. “Think about it. And then you’ll understand and accept my offer to help you, and the child inside you, willingly.”

He touches the tip of his boot to my car’s tire and I watch as it slowly reinflates. “If you apply enough pressure to an object—or a person—from every direction,” he says, “it will always collapse and give you what you want. But when you release the pressure, there can be a recovery … of sorts.” He looks into my eyes. “I hope you make the wise choice, Declan.” Then he walks away.

Chapter Twenty-Four

By the time I reach Alexander's house, I feel as though I can't breathe. I didn't call him from the car because I was stunned and reeling and I wanted to convince myself that everything Malentus said was lies, but all I managed to do was spin myself up further. When Alexander opens the door, he sees the look on my face and folds me into his arms. I feel a flood of his energy pouring over me, gradually soothing my ragged insides so I can remember how to find my center and calm my racing heart.

"It's okay, it's okay, you're here with me," he says over and over as he holds me. "What happened?" he asks and I can see the intensity of the worry in his eyes. He walks me over to the couch in the living room and sits me down next to him and, as he holds my hands, I manage to spill out everything, relaying every detail.

"Is it true?" I ask, emotions overflowing. I can't help think that if this is something Alexander has been keeping from me I won't ever be able to forgive him. Not this time.

"No, Declan, no," he says vehemently. "It can't be. He said it to plant doubt in your mind. It's a trick."

"But what if it *is* true? What if I *am* his daughter? And our baby is his grandchild?"

He shakes his head resolutely. "I'll never believe that. You could no more be Malentus's daughter than I could. You're pure goodness, Declan. Through and through. I feel it. I'd know if part of you was as dark as Malentus." He looks into my eyes. "Our child was created with pure love. It's a child that's going to change the world—for the forces of good, not evil. Malentus knows that. He's trying to make you have doubts so you'll fall into his trap. He's desperate to keep the baby from ever being born."

"Would you tell me the truth?" I ask, searching his eyes. "Even if it were true? You haven't been keeping this from me?"

"Declan," he says, meeting my gaze, "I learned my lesson. I would never keep anything like that from you ever again. I promise you, with every fiber of my being, that I would tell you if I knew this to be true. But it isn't. It's all lies meant to cause you anguish and make you doubt. He wants you to trust him. And follow him. So he can hurt you and our child."

"But how do you *know*?" I say with a rush of emotion. "My mom said she dated Malcolm. And she became pregnant with me right after, when she was with my dad—so the timing is possible. Even if she didn't sleep with Malentus willingly, something could have happened in Nusquam. She doesn't remember anything. How would we even know? Maybe that's why my dad gave away his power. Not just because he loved my mom but so he could make sure that he and my mom raised me, instead of Malentus." I look up into Alexander's eyes. "That would explain why I have powers even though my dad didn't. Maybe my power is evil power, from Malentus." My words flow out as a surging stream of jumbled thoughts and distress. "How do you know he's not telling the truth?"

"I know, Declan," he says, looking deep into my eyes, "because I know you. Inside and out. And I know your power. It's *good*. Like you are. Do you trust me? Do you trust that I would know if this were true? Please don't let him get inside your head. This is their game. They drop bombs and plant doubt and watch the ensuing mayhem from the sidelines with glee. I know you. And I love you. And I'm telling you, you bring light to the world, not darkness. And I know in my heart our child will bring pure light, too."

I nod, wanting to believe him. But from direct experience I know that Avestan, and now Malentus, are artful at planting seeds of doubt and waiting for the malicious tendrils of suspicion to take root and grow.

In a small corner of my mind disquiet gives way to misgiving and I wonder if I can ever feel fully certain of anything ever again.

Chapter Twenty-Five

Edwin arrives home as we're talking and Alexander and I fill him in. He reacts with an instant of shocked horror followed by a response so swift and sure that it makes me feel hopeful.

"Declan," he says, leaning forward as he sits in his reading chair next to the couch where I'm sitting, "I don't believe this is true for a moment. It's a desperate, vicious lie meant to trick you or at least leave you dreadfully unsteady and I'm sorry that it seems to be working." He reaches over to squeeze my hand as he looks at me before continuing. "But you need to understand something … because I can see in your eyes that you're carrying some doubt. Even if it *were* true, your physical mixture of molecules and atoms don't make you who you are. It's what's inside your heart. And I see what Alexander sees and every other guardian who protects you sees. You are light and beauty and kindness and you're *good*. It's in your eyes and it's in the way you carry yourself in the world and treat those around you. The universe is a better place for having your soul in it. And I've said it before, but I firmly believe it: your child is going to change the world. For the better. I'm certain of that."

His words and the surety behind them cause a lump to form in my throat, and as I look into his eyes I can see the sincerity resting there. I had no idea that was how Edwin thought of me. He squeezes my hand again and I can't keep myself from standing up and giving him a giant, sloppy hug for his warmth and kindness.

As comforted as I am, however, my mind keeps replaying one part of what he said: *"even if it were true"* like a turntable needle stuck in a groove. Edwin, unlike Alexander, hasn't discounted the possibility outright, and that leaves me feeling quietly unsettled, despite what he said about molecules and atoms.

It's beginning to sink in, distressingly, that I may never be free from some measure of doubt.

"Do you want to postpone the wedding?" Alexander asks me as we lie in bed in his room with morning sunlight peeking in the blinds. We fell asleep in each other's arms last night, fully clothed, on top of his bed, as he held me and tried to reassure me over and over that everything Malentus told me was all lies. It was only in the middle of the night that we awoke and finally got undressed and under the covers together—the state we're in now.

"What? No, of course not," I say. I lift my head off his chest to look into his eyes. "I've been looking forward to this and counting down the days."

He leans over and kisses me. "Me, too. But I would understand if you want some time to process everything's that been thrown at you."

I shake my head. "All along I've had this fear that our wedding day would never come and now that it's finally almost here there's no way I'll let Malentus or Avestan or any other dark guardian ruin it."

“Okay,” he says with a broad smile, “because in less than 36 hours’ time it *will* be here. I’ll spend the day today getting everything ready and we’ll have the rehearsal tonight and then tomorrow we do it.”

“We *do it*?” I laugh. “You’re usually so eloquent.”

“I think I’m actually nervous,” he says.

I meet his eyes. “That’s sweet.”

“I love you,” he says with a smile. “More than you know. You’re not the only one who feared this day would never come.”

I stretch up to give him a kiss, basking in the way our energies weave and blend together. Then I rest my head on his warm, hard chest again and we lie in companionable silence for a long while until eventually I turn my head and look at the clock. “We should probably think about getting up soon,” I say without much conviction.

He groans in protest. “I want to hold you a little while longer,” he says as he pulls me closer and kisses me softly.

As I lie in the safety of Alexander’s arms, enjoying that familiar spark and the way our energy flows in blissful harmony, I’m almost able to believe that our wedding, and the birth of our baby, will both go forward without harm from dark guardians.

If only I could escape the memory of Malentus’s cold, dead eyes.

Chapter Twenty-Six

My mom helps me lift the dress over my head one last time before the wedding tomorrow to make any final adjustments. She ties the string of the halter neckline at the back of my neck, exposing my bare shoulders, and secures the waist above my baby bump with the long built-in sash. The white, flowing sundress didn't even require any hemming in the end. My baby bump rose it up in front and its slightly longer drape in back gently sweeps the ground as if it was planned that way all along. I turn and look in the mirror as my mom places the woven circlet of sparse white forget-me-nots over the long waves of my hair, slightly back, like a crown. The white, flowing lines of the dress, combined with the woven flower crown and the dewy glow of being eight months pregnant, all coalesce to furnish an effect of a blue-eyed fairy queen stepped straight from the forest. I imagine myself with Alexander tomorrow in our fairy ring of sweeping redwoods and I smile. With heart full to overflowing I meet my mom's eyes in the mirror.

"It's perfect," I say.

My mom answers with tears in her eyes. "You look beautiful, Declan. So beautiful."

I turn around to hug her and she holds me tight and kisses me on the forehead. "I can't believe my baby's getting married," she says.

"And having a baby," I add.

"That, too," she says. "You've had a busy year."

I laugh. "Too much?"

She shakes her head. "Declan, I want you to know that I love Alexander and I see how happy he makes you. And I see how hard you're working at school and how much you both love and want this baby. I couldn't be prouder of the woman you've become or feel happier for the life you're building together. And the fact that you're wearing my wedding dress touches my heart more deeply than you'll ever know. I know your dad will be watching tomorrow with as much love and happiness as I'll be feeling."

I wipe the tears from my eyes and hug her again. "Thanks, mom," I say, my voice thick with emotion.

The doorbell rings and we pause in our moment together. "That's Liz," I say. "She told me she's coming over to see the dress."

I bound down the stairs (as quickly as any woman in her last month of pregnancy can bound down anything, which is actually pretty slowly, to be honest) and as I yank open the front door with a wide smile I say, "What do you think?"

Only instead of Liz waiting for me on the doorstep, it's Alexander.

His expression is stunned as his eyes travel over me and his face softens with what I can only describe as a heart-melting expression of awe mixed with adoration. "I think you're the most beautiful woman I've ever seen," he breathes as he meets my eyes.

I smile and my eyes get watery because I know he means it—because in that moment, I can not only feel the string of light that connects our hearts together, I can almost see it, and it's filling me with warmth and overwhelming love. "You're not supposed to see the bride in her dress before the wedding," I say quietly, almost shyly.

"I don't believe in superstitions," he says with a smile.

"I was going for the fairy queen look," I say.

He smiles, his green eyes crinkling in that irresistible way of his. "Mission accomplished."

I laugh.

"You're the most beautiful fairy queen there ever was," he adds.

"You really like it?"

"Words cannot express how much I like it."

I smile. "Why do I feel shy right now?"

"Because we're getting married tomorrow and you're in your wedding dress and you weren't expecting to see me at the door."

"I thought you were Liz."

"I assumed," he says with a smile. "But I love how you smiled when you realized it was me—the way you always smile when you see me. And the way your eyes light up, so blue and vivid, and gorgeous."

My smile grows. "I can't help it. It's how you make me feel." *My heart does somersaults when he's around, what can I say?* "But I thought you were getting things ready all day?"

"I am. I'm heading over there now but I stopped by because I remembered I needed to do something first."

"What?"

"This." He steps forward and pulls me into his arms and kisses me, taking me by surprise. His lips are soft on mine at first and then more ardent as the kiss deepens. I thread my fingers in his hair as he holds me against him and then, all too soon, he steps back, leaving me breathless.

"I missed you," he says.

"*That's* what you remembered you needed to do?"

He smiles. "Yes."

"I just left your house an hour ago," I say wryly.

"And?' he says, "Your point is?"

"No point," I smile, "I missed you, too."

He laughs. "I promise I'll go now." He starts to leave and then he turns back and dips me dramatically and kisses me one more time and we both laugh. As he walks away again, he pauses at the door and turns back one last time and traces a path around me with his eyes before he blinks once, slowly.

"What are you doing?" I ask.

"Taking a picture of you in my mind."

I smile, heart swelling in my chest. "Why?"

"Because you're beautiful," he says, almost in a whisper, his voice a mixture of wonder and tender sincerity, "and I want to remember this moment. For eternity."

My eyes get misty again. “I love you,” I say softly.

“I love you, too,” he says. “I’ll see you at five.”

Chapter Twenty-Seven

I drive my mom's car along the gravel road to where Alexander and I always park near the ranger station in the back of Redwood Park. His car is already here. Then I text Alexander to let him know I arrived and I start along the winding footpath that will take me to our fairy ring in the forest. I know it's a state park but I consider it "ours" anyway because of our initials in the remains of the redwood tree in the center.

I changed into jeans (with expansion fabric that my mom sewed in for me in the front) and a cute, sky-blue empire waist top that ties in the back. Within less than a minute Alexander meets me on the path and I can't help but stare, nearly dazed, at the sight of him standing tall, dark and knee-weakening-ly handsome before me.

He's wearing a slate gray suit and crisp white dress shirt with a rich blue tie. The suit traces his athletic frame to perfection and the dark gray color offsets his deep green eyes. The way he's standing, with one hand casually in his pants pocket, makes him look like a model posed in a catalogue. He rakes the fingers of his other hand through his thick, dark hair a little self-consciously. "You like it?" he asks.

I can barely speak. "I think you're the most handsome man in the world," I say when I gather my voice.

He smiles. "Since I saw you in your dress I thought it was only fair that you should see me in my suit."

"I like the cobalt tie," I say.

"I like your descriptive names for colors," he says, and I laugh.

"The tie was inspired by your aura," he adds. "But I'm sure you guessed that."

I nod, smiling, and sigh. "You know, other than the fact that we both have dark angels hellbent on killing us, I feel like the luckiest girl in the world."

He laughs. "Always the optimist."

I trace my eyes over him from head to toe, taking him in once more. "You really are devastatingly handsome," I say.

"I'm glad you think so," he says with a rakish smile. "I'd let you take advantage of me on this path right now but the sun's going down soon and we still need to rehearse."

I laugh and he sweeps me up in his arms and carries me effortlessly along the path to our destination. When we get close, he covers my eyes. "Don't turn around yet," he says as he sets me down in front of him, facing away from the fairy ring. He rolls his shoulders and straightens his shirt cuffs the way he always does, like James Bond after a skirmish, and I smile and swear to God he's so handsome I think I may faint. "Okay," he says, "now you can turn around."

I turn around slowly and when I see the ring of towering redwoods my hand flutters to my heart. Alexander has decorated it with blue and white lights wrapped in the trees the same way he did when we first kissed and he asked me to marry him. Only now, white folding chairs are set up on either side of a middle aisle, marked by a long stretch of white fabric and leading to a beautiful rustic arch perched over our initials. Strings of blue and white Forget-Me-Nots are entwined throughout the woven wood branches of the arch. It's gorgeous and magical and I don't have words for how utterly perfect it is.

I meet Alexander's eyes. "I love it," I whisper, my heart swollen in my chest.

"Third time's a charm," he says with a smile. "These lights worked for us so well, twice before, that I figured they were lucky."

"I thought you weren't superstitious," I say.

He smiles. "I also know you like them." He slides his fingers into mine and leads me over to the arch. "I thought you could walk down this admittedly very short aisle and we could stand here," he says, "on our initials, when we take our vows."

"That sounds perfect."

"Should we rehearse?" he asks.

"Sure. Do we have a lot to rehearse?"

He laughs. "Not really, I think we've gone over everything. It's just me and you, and Edwin performing the ceremony, and family and friends watching. I'll have the champagne and sparkling water here on ice with the champagne glasses."

"And you have the music ready?"

"Vivaldi's *Spring*."

"And the playlist we put together for after the ceremony?"

He nods. "Complete with *At Last* for our first dance."

I smile. "I have good memories dancing with you to that song," I say, remembering our first kiss.

"Me, too," he says softly. "I also added *Powerful* to our playlist, by the way."

"You did?" I smile.

He nods. "I listened to it so many times during those weeks when you wouldn't see me, I'm surprised I don't despise it. But I've come to think of it as our song. One of them, anyway."

I meet his eyes and smile. "I honestly didn't think it was possible, but the thought of you sitting and listening to that song over and over and thinking of us just made me love you even more."

He laughs. "I shouldn't have told you."

"No, I love that song," I say. "And I think of us whenever I hear it, too. I love that you told me." I lean over and kiss him sweetly and he smiles.

"What should we do to rehearse?" I ask, "Should we go over our vows?"

"I thought we'd save them to surprise each other tomorrow. But we could practice with the rings now and do a little ad lib."

"Ad lib?" I laugh, "This isn't much of a rehearsal."

He smiles with a glint in his eyes. "Maybe it was just a pretext to get you out here alone."

I push his arm. "I love that we'll basically be winging it tomorrow," I say with a grin. "But tonight can be like our own private wedding ceremony."

He smiles and reaches into his pocket and pulls out my platinum wedding band. "I know we wanted to keep it simple but I added something to your band."

Intrigued, I lift it out of his hand and hold it up to look closer and when I see the engraving on the inside, tears spring to my eyes. In a simple, yet elegant script along the inside of the band he engraved *A.R. loves D.J. Always.*

I look up and meet his eyes and wrap my arms around him and kiss him. "I can't believe you did this," I whisper.

"You don't like it?" he asks.

I shake my head as I lean over to my purse I set down on one of the chairs and pull out his platinum wedding band and hand it to him. He holds it up and when he notices the engraving on the inside of the band, he meets my eyes. "You did the same thing?"

I nod. Along the inside of his band I had the jeweler engrave *D.J. loves A.R. Always.*

He smiles and kisses me. "More proof that we were made for each other." He takes the ring from my hand and gazes into my eyes as he slips it onto my finger. "I, Alexander Ronin, take you, Declan Jane, as my wife, to have and to hold, to love and adore, for endless time and eons beyond. You are the tomato soup to my jaffle and you make my soul sing."

I laugh. "The tomato soup to your jaffle?"

"My two favorite things that go better together. They enhance each other, like we do," he says with a smile. "And you've stated, many times, that jaffle is your favorite word."

I laugh again and smile back, holding his gaze, and slip his ring on his finger. "I, Declan Jane, take you, Alexander Ronin, as my husband, to have and to hold, to love and adore, to laugh with and talk with and just enjoy *being* with, for eternity and beyond. You are the strawberry jelly to my peanut butter and you make my soul sing, too."

He laughs. "I'm jam?"

"My favorite kind," I smile.

We stare into the depths of one another's eyes and continue to smile and then he caresses my cheek as he smooths away a stray lock of hair, and we kiss, under our wedding arch, as the sun's rays line up in the sky, *just so*, and shine a beam of light upon us.

"So we can leave this all here?" I ask as we're getting ready to leave the fairy ring. We've been talking and kissing for so long that the sun is low in the sky now and the wind is kicking up.

"Believe it or not, I actually pursued official permission this time," he says. "No one's ever asked to be married here before, apparently. It's too far up in the forest I guess, so it took some sorting, but they agreed in the end after I signed a load of legal forms and paid the required fees along with a hefty deposit. They even included the ranger cart to tote everyone up and back."

I smile. "Even angels have to pay deposits."

"But we always get them back," he says, and I laugh.

"I can't believe that tomorrow at this time we'll be married," I say.

He smiles. "Do you want us to spend tonight apart? The night before our wedding?"

"Is that what you want?"

"Honestly? No."

I laugh. "That wasn't what I was expecting from the King of Planning and Anticipation."

"Believe me there'll be plenty of plans in our future," he says. "Plans that involve a tremendous amount of anticipation. But right now I'm feeling like I want to savor every minute I have with you. If you'd rather we spend the night apart, though, I understand."

I shake my head. "I want to sleep next to you. Tonight and every night."

He kisses me and I melt into his arms again, enjoying the sensation of feeling his lips on mine and just basking in the feeling of being together. When we draw back, his eyes stray to something over my shoulder and his expression changes. I look behind me but don't see anything.

"It's starting to get dark," he says. "We should go."

"Can you fly us back?" I ask. The idea of flying right now as light energy with Alexander would be the perfect ending to the time we just spent together. He surprises me, however, by declining.

"I'll carry you," he says. "It'll be a fast walk. I want to preserve my energy for tomorrow."

When we reach the small gravel lot near the ranger station Alexander gives me a kiss and opens the door for me to get into my mom's car. "I'll meet you back at your house in a tick."

"You're not leaving now?"

"I have something left to do back at the ring. I'll be along later."

I look over at his car parked next to mine. "Okay," I say. "Don't take too long."

He nods. "Watch for me," he says. Then, as I start to drive away he puts his hand on my car to stop me.

"What is it?" I ask, worried.

He leans down through the open window and clutches my face in his hands and kisses me, hard, surprising me. The kiss goes on and on, and I sense the fervency behind it and I entwine my fingers in his hair and kiss him back, just as ardently, and it's as if we're drowning together in the intensity of feeling between us. When he finally draws back, leaving me breathless, he gazes into my eyes. "I love you," he breathes. "Watch for me."

I nod but as I turn the car around and drive down the gravel road and onto the highway toward home, something in his words, "*Watch for me,*" leaves me uneasy. It's an odd turn of phrase, and as I roll it over and over in my mind a knot begins to form in the pit of my stomach.

Chapter Twenty-Eight
Alexander

I walk back to the fairy ring and go over and over in my mind, as I have a thousand times, all the different ways this can play out. I thought, *hoped,* I had loads of time to be with Declan—eternity, really. But I've been around long enough to know that hopes and dreams are never guaranteed and this may not resolve with the fairytale ending I wanted.

When I arrive, he steps out from the trees where I spotted him earlier when he was watching me with Declan.

"Alexander," he says matter-of-factly.

"Malentus."

We stare at each other in silence for a long while. I noticed a limp when he strode into the clearing and now, as he stands tall, I can see that he's favoring his left side. I embrace a measure of satisfaction at the idea that these injuries are residual from the beating I gave him the last time we met, but I know better than that. The wounds I was able to inflict on Malentus surely healed a long time ago. I wish I could say the same about the damage he inflicted on me. Instinctively, I touch my side where the scar is.

"I was hoping this could wait until after the wedding," I say.

"If wishes were horses," Malentus says with an air of fatalism that I always knew was coming. "I allowed the guardians surrounding you to believe that they were strong enough to hold me back, but I was only waiting for the proper time to intercede. They put up a good fight, though—tougher than expected. Unfortunately for you and Declan, however, it wasn't good enough."

"Intercede for who? Avestan?"

"The important point for you to understand," he says, "is that the deal we strike here today will be honored by Avestan. I'm the only one who can keep him in line, in fact. I'm sure you know how disobedient and impulsive children can be." He frames the words with an air of dismissive annoyance.

"Impulsive? You mean my brother? Who you turned against me?"

"Surely you know I can only make a man blossom into what was already inside."

"I'm not making any deals with you."

He sighs heavily. "If you only knew how many times I've heard those words. It's interesting the deals people make—even guardians—when they have no choice."

"There's always a choice."

"Let's assume that's true. I'll give you nearly the same choice I gave Declan's father all those years ago: I'll make you a mortal—so you can live a wretched mortal's life with your little sprite girlfriend—all you have to do is give me your power and my grandchild."

"We both know it's not your grandchild," I say.

"Let's not pretend we know anything for certain. It comes down to a matter of trading the baby in exchange for

Declan's life. What I do with the child is no concern of yours."

"What you do with *my* child is no concern of mine? You can't possibly think I would make any sort of deal with you."

"Let me be clearer," he says forcefully. "Option B is that everyone dies. Is that a better solution? Or would you rather save Declan? I'm offering the opportunity for you to live a mortal life with her. Isn't that what she always wanted? For you to grow old together? To live a *normal* life? Now's your chance to give her what she truly wants. What she deserves, really. Think about it, Alexander. This overture I'm making is more than generous. Avestan won't like it, but I'm the only one who can ensure he stands by it."

"The way you stood by it with Declan's father? You killed him anyway and you used his best friend as the weapon."

"Mortals are weak," he says with a shrug. "And when you find the right ones they're astonishingly predictable. It took some time, but her father's law partner turned out to have quite flexible morals. Multiple nudges, sustained over time, was all it took. You could almost say it wasn't my fault."

It disgusts me to listen to him talk about the murder of Declan's father as if it were a parlor game. "There's only one deal I'll make," I say. "You and Avestan, and Alenna if she's with you, leave San Mar now, and leave Declan and the baby alone. Forever. For that, I won't destroy you."

"Is that a joke?" Malentus asks mockingly. "You're forgetting, Alexander, that you have no leverage."

"My leverage is that you're wounded. I saw you limp out from the trees and you're clearly favoring your left side. You may have made it past our guardians, but you said yourself it was far more difficult than you envisioned, and now you're at a disadvantage. You're weakened, Malentus. And vulnerable."

His eyes narrow. "I'll remind you that I'm an ancient. I'm faster than you and I'm vastly stronger and more powerful. I know you felt that, acutely, the last time we met. Yet you foolishly chose to skirmish with me anyway and you paid the price. How does that long, jagged scar on your side feel every morning when you wake up? Is it tight on your skin? Do you feel how deep it goes? I could suffer a thousand more wounds like the ones I received today and I'd still be able to destroy you without taking a full breath. You have no leverage, Alexander, trust me."

"What's that old saying about protesting too much?"

"You're bluffing," Malentus says.

"Try me. You know what I can do, and I'm not going down without a fight."

"This is your last chance, Alexander." His voice is flat and menacing. "My offer still stands for exactly thirty seconds only: you, living a mortal life with your precious sprite, in exchange for your energy and the child."

I hold his gaze, silent, as the seconds tick by.

"So be it," Malentus says, heaving an onerous sigh. "Everyone dies."

I brace myself as he sends a bolt of black light aimed at my chest. I manage to dodge it and instead of predictably throwing my energy from the distance between us, I rush him instead, kneeing him hard in the groin and punching him so forcefully I can feel his orbital ridge crumble under my fist. If I have any hope of beating him I have to fight hard and fight dirty. He can heal the surface wounds, I know, but they still cause pain and they may provide the distraction I need to strike him with my energy before he can block me.

I kick him hard while he's on the ground and send a cannonball of light straight to his wretched, evil heart. It hits and I send another and another, and as I'm holding him down, for a brief, beautiful moment I let myself believe that maybe Malentus *is* wounded more than he let on. Perhaps this isn't futile and I can keep Declan and the baby safe and still be with them and we can have the life together I imagined … the life I crave so desperately and imagined so many times. I allow myself to believe, in this moment, the starry-eyed notion that it's possible for me to win against one of the most powerful dark guardians in existence.

I hold that belief in my mind as I keep hitting Malentus with everything I've got. With colossal force I send bolt after bolt of surging white light straight into his cold, black heart. I don't keep anything in reserve. I wasn't bluffing when I said I won't go down without a fight. If I can't obliterate the evil in front of me, I'll die trying. There's no other way.

As I draw on every ounce of power, I focus on my love for Declan, and indulge myself with the idea that maybe it hasn't really come down to this—to what I dreaded all along.

I stare at Malentus, still on the ground, and I continue to strike him, over and over, with brutal, unrelenting force as I hold him with my light, and in the moment that I start to believe, really *believe* that I may have a chance, he slowly manages to stand up … and then he laughs.

He meets my eyes with his cold, black stare and crushes the final remnant of hope I held close.

When the dark flash of light hits me, I'm knocked off my feet and the searing pain I feel as it burns through to my soul tells me what I already know: this is the end.

If I'm going to do what I hoped I'd never have to, it's now or never. Soon, I won't have enough power left within me.

I attempt to rise and thick fear takes hold when I can't move. But I *have* to. I summon all the love I feel for Declan and our child and I imagine her smile and her laugh and the way she looks at me when I come into a room. Then I imagine her aura, and the vibrancy of the blues and the brilliant whites that surround her, and I remember how it makes me feel when we're together. I sense my life force fading and I know I have to summon the power to do this or she'll never be safe. I rise up, picturing Declan's arm outstretched for me, lifting me off the ground, so I can do what Malentus never expected. I feel him hitting me with everything he has. He's risking himself to prove to me how superior he is, how much more power he wields, just as I always knew he would. And this is my chance.

Instead of resisting I embrace all the evil he's directing into me and with every ounce of light I have left I merge our energy into one. Malentus forged this connection to me and I'm certain he never thought I'd have the will or the power to turn it back on him. But he vastly underestimated the love I feel for Declan and what I'm willing to do to protect her and our child.

I may not have the power to defeat him outright and remain here to be with Declan, but I'll fight like hell to take him with me, even if it means I'll be gone forever.

"*This* is my leverage," I hiss into his ear and I can feel his surprise and sudden resistance, but when I sense his growing fear becoming one with me—cold and vile and searingly malevolent—I know that it's working.

Declan and our baby will be safe.

In my final moments, before our energy transforms and escapes into the universe, I grip the note I left in my pocket, just in case, and as my final act as Alexander Ronin, I send my mortal shell to Declan with light.

To try to explain.

Chapter Twenty-Nine

I can't shake this uneasy feeling.

And the farther I drive, the more it transforms into mounting dread. I'm halfway home but I pull over and turn the car around.

Something is terribly wrong. I feel it.

As I drive back toward Redwood Park and the fairy ring where I left Alexander, the dread hits me like a bolt of electricity, making me step on the gas. I drive down the gravel access road and when I see Alexander's car, still there, without him around, I feel panic rising in my throat.

I step out of my car, into a fierce, blowing gale, and that's when I hear Alexander's voice, carried on the wind.

Watch for me.

I look up and my heart lifts to the sky because I see him at the entrance to the trail, and he's waving to me.

But my feeling of relief disappears almost instantly. Something isn't right. I can see it in the sadness in his eyes or maybe it's his wave, or the way he's not shining brightly from within, as he always does.

And then, as my brain struggles to process this disparate information, it becomes clear that something *is* wrong. Terribly wrong. Because now, before my eyes, Alexander's body crumples to the ground. And the way he crumples, like a lifeless doll, without any attempt to break his fall, sends my heart plummeting through my center and drives my soul outside of my body as I run, nearly tripping over myself, to try to catch him.

But when I reach him on the ground and lift his head into my lap my hand recoils because his skin is already cold. So cold. And lifeless. I've lost my voice and I'm losing my mind because this can't be.

This can't be Alexander lying lifeless in my lap on the eve of our wedding.

This can't be how it ends.

Tears come and I kiss him over and over. I kiss his forehead and his lips and his cheeks and his lips again and again and again, trying to warm him and renew his life force. I lift his hands to kiss those, too, and that's when I see the folded piece of stationery gripped in his palm with *Declan* written on the outside.

My hands are shaking as I slide it out of his fingers and unfold it, and my tears fall on the paper, causing the ink to blur and bleed, as I read the words Alexander left behind.

My Dearest Declan,

If you're reading this, I'm sorry. More sorry than words can ever convey. Please know this wasn't my plan. I said I would do anything to protect you and the baby and I gave it all I had but my plan didn't work.

I was forced to do something I didn't want to. Something I hoped it would never come to.

I did it for you, and I did it for our child, and also for the world that our child is going to bring so much light into and make a better place.

Malentus can no longer hurt you. And Edwin promised me he'd protect you from Avestan—in the same manner, if it comes to it.

I want to say that my heart is broken over how this ended, but I think my heart is the only part of me that will live on, so I don't want it to be broken. And I don't want your heart to be broken either. Please find a way to go on and live a happy life with our child. I want you to smile when you think of me ... and when you think of us ... and what we had.

Please don't let thoughts of me bring you only sadness. I couldn't bear it.

If there's a possibility for my energy to communicate with you, you know I'll do whatever it takes to break through, so watch for me. Souls with a connection as deep as ours have a way of finding each other across time and space and I hope that's true for us, in any form. I'll never stop searching. I think if I didn't believe there was some small chance to connect with you again, no matter how remote, I wouldn't have been able to do what I did. After all, what we had is more powerful than anything I ever dreamed of, or thought possible.

I love you, Declan. Deeply and always. Into eternity and eons beyond.

True love like ours never ends.

Alexander

Teardrops continue to fall in a silent, broken rhythm as I struggle, in shock, to accept the finality of Alexander's words. I won't do it. I won't. I don't accept it. I kiss him again and again, lips slick with tears, just as I did when he was lifeless in my arms once before. But he remains cold, not moving, and deep down I sense the futility of my attempts. Nothing can change this, no matter what sprite powers I can summon or how much I want to tear the fabric of the universe open with my bare hands and make it not true.

The door to the life I imagined and dreamed of so many times with Alexander has closed forever and I'm left with only wrenching, heartaching despair.

I rock Alexander in my arms over and over as I sob in agony until my lungs have ceased taking in air and no sound can get out. I continue to cry, silently, until a sharp pain in my lower back shocks me into focusing on a new and different type of agony. The sharp pain is followed by a forceful contraction that wracks my body and leaves me gasping.

Oh my God, the baby is coming.

But it's too early.

A dark shroud of dread falls over me as I sense a presence in the woods.

I turn, slowly, to see Avestan smiling wickedly, enjoying the sight before him.

Chapter Thirty

"*You did this,*" I whisper vilely, the words clawing from my throat like tiny daggers. I feel another contraction building within me but it can't compete with the misery and fury I'm directing at Avestan in this moment.

Avestan laughs. "Alexander sacrificed himself? To save you? How quaint, and selfless, and *thick.*"

"He took your Maker with him," I spit out.

He shrugs, unfazed. "Malentus was willing to cut a deal. A deal I disagreed with, most vehemently. But it turns out Alexander's sacrifice was all for naught. Because here I am, ready to destroy you and your baby after all."

"You'll be weakened now," I say with a measure of satisfaction. "Your Maker is gone."

He shrugs again and flexes his hands in the air. "Strong as ever," he says. "They say it takes quite a while to make its way throughout the line. But consider this—perhaps it's only a myth we spread to entice the guardians to sacrifice themselves. Like the stupid lemmings they are."

"You're lying," I say threateningly. "I can see the fear and dread in your eyes. And Edwin's coming for you."

"The only thing you can see in my eyes is the delight at what I'm about to do to you, to end this. And I wouldn't count on Edwin. Alenna's keeping him busy for me. I was just there, cheering her on in fact."

I look down at Alexander in my arms and my heart is so drained that part of me wants to give up and tell Avestan to kill me now and be done with it. I can't take it anymore. I want out of this torment and searing grief. But another contraction rips through me, causing me to gasp in pain, and I'm reminded of the life growing inside of me—the life fighting to come out—and I know I can't give up.

"What's this?" Avestan says as steps forward and rips Alexander's letter out of my hand. As he pulls away the fragile paper, wet with my tears, it falls into pieces, and that's when I truly break.

And something in me snaps.

Rage swells within my chest, to a level and degree I've never felt before, and as it threatens to consume me whole, I gently lower Alexander's head from my lap to the ground and stand up, slowly, a quiet fire engulfing my insides.

I turn to Avestan with a voice as bitter as acid. "*You did this.*" My hand thrusts forward with all the fury in my heart and a ray of light bursts from it and strikes Avestan's chest with explosive precision and intensity. He falls to the ground, momentarily stunned, before unleashing his own flash of black light in my direction. When it hits, the pain is excruciating but somehow welcome, because it distracts me from the real agony underneath.

"*You did this,*" I say again, my voice steeped in stinging, vicious despair. I keep up my assault on Avestan, sending wave after pulsing wave of searing white light directly into his miserable, shriveled heart and I will it to stop beating from the strength of my wrath alone. And I can feel it working … but at the same time I feel his energy draining my life force, too … only I won't stop, I *can't* stop, because if this is my last stand, I'll use every last breath to save my baby and take Avestan with me. Another contraction rips through my body and I use the pain to hit Avestan again with everything I've got.

"Stop!"

We both hear Alenna's voice and turn to see her standing to the right of us, eyes wide with panic, at the spectacle in front of her.

"Avestan!" she cries out in horror. "Alexander is dead! He's gone—forever. You got what you wanted. Yet you're killing yourself! Why won't you *stop*?"

"She has to die, too," Avestan hisses, not letting up on the bolt of black light he's burning into me. "Alexander will feel her death, wherever he is. He has to know that *I* won."

I feel Alenna's rage ripple out in almost visible waves that roll over us with white-hot intensity. "Alexander was obsessed with her," she spits out acidly, "so obsessed that he died for her! And now you are, too! You're going to destroy yourself! But *I'm* here," she pleads, "the girl you said you loved—the one you killed for … and we can be together now. Forever. Are you going to throw that all away? Because of *her*?" Her voice fades and her eyes fix on me and then flick back to Avestan with a look of hurt so wide and so deep that I feel it swallowing her from within.

But Avestan doesn't back down from the fatal duel we're locked in and I can feel Alenna's fury spill over as she realizes that he's not going to stop.

Not even for her.

She looks at Avestan, burning his black light into me, and then she looks at me as I continue to fight back with my own light, and when her eyes meet mine I feel her contempt and her fury but also something else … *regret?*

I don't sense the pain anymore. I'm beyond that now, and as Avestan's beam of black light burns through me, and I prepare to take what I know will be my final breath, fighting for my baby, I watch as Alenna does something wholly unexpected. She rushes Avestan and she holds him to her, and I see him resisting but he won't stop burning his light into me. I sense he can't fight off Alenna at the same time that he's killing me, but, still, he *won't stop*—not until he knows he's won. I feel him doubling down on the energy he's sending into me, shooting a fiery bolt with explosive force that pierces the center of my heart with searing precision. My heartbeat jolts and then slows, until gradually I sense the wounds are too great … and I know this is the end. I see her light enter his body and embrace his darkness and, with hazy amazement, I watch as their bodies start to transform before my eyes and spiral upwards, into the air.

And the last thing I see, before I take my final breath, is Edwin running towards me. His eyes follow mine up to the night sky where the spiral that was once Avestan and Alenna transforms into what can only be described as a beautiful shooting star.

Chapter Thirty-One

The Hospital

I see my mom first. She's in the waiting room, crying, and Mark has his arm around her, looking grave. I can feel his deep love for her, and for me, and the fear in his heart—borne of painful, lasting memories of receiving bad news in hospitals, years ago, when his wife had cancer. I've never tuned into Chief Stephens in this way before and it brings me peace as I feel his bright aura and his devotion to my mom and the comfort they bring each other.

My mom. *Oh,* my mom.

The love between us glows like a bright golden sun filling the room. I send her a wave of warm white light to buoy her heart and remind her how much I love her. She looks up for a brief moment, but soon she puts her head back down in her hands and begins to cry again, silently.

The doctor walks in and she and Mark stand up and I hear her ask the doctor a question and I see the doctor shake his head and I hear her begin to sob and collapse into Mark's arms as he holds her against him.

"What about the baby?" I hear someone ask. And this time I can feel that the doctor's answer is a salve to my mother's wounded heart.

"The baby survived, miraculously," I hear the doctor say, and I grasp pieces of their conversation: *It's a girl. Healthy and fully developed despite being nearly a month premature. Your daughter was a fighter, Mrs. Jane. I think she gave her last breath to ensure the baby survived .... I'm so sorry for your loss .... There was nothing more we could do .... You say it was dry lightning? I've only seen one other case like it before with those kinds of injuries ...*

"Edwin saw it happen," my mom answers through her tears as she turns her head to look behind her and that's when I notice that Edwin is also in the room, sitting off to the side, staring into the middle distance, his face full of anguish. "He said it struck them both as they were standing together … he found them in each other's arms on the ground …. They were supposed to be married tomorrow …." My mom's voice drifts off and she begins to sob again in Mark's arms as he holds her tight with tears escaping his eyes, too.

"Yes," Edwin confirms quietly. "That's what it was." He's silent for a moment and then he adds, almost too softly to hear, his words steeped in anguish, "I was too late … I was too late to help."

I've never seen Edwin cry before. I can feel his aura, bathed in sorrow, and I want to tell him that it's okay. I'm here. But I sense that he already knows that … he's crying for all that was lost.

I watch everything with a curious detachment. I feel no pain, only deep, abiding love, and as I peer into their sadness I have a vision into the future of a day when they'll all be happy again.

I see my mom holding a baby girl with my golden hair and Alexander's deep emerald eyes. And I know it's going to be okay because Mark is there, too, beside my mom with his arm around her, and Finn and Liz and Edwin are also there, and they all smile at Miracle Jane Alexandra Ronin (Mira for short), which my mom named her, as I told her I was planning to do.

And I see visions farther into the future with my mom and Mark raising Mira and experiencing many happy days, and Finn and Liz taking Mira to the park when she's older, and she's calling them Aunt Liz and Uncle Finn and she's laughing, and so are they as they swing her up in the air between them as they walk, holding hands. And Edwin—Edwin is ever present in Mira's life, too, and I feel his protective, comforting aura surrounding her from near and far. He smiles every time he looks at her.

And in every vision I see, Mira smiles back at all of them with an unmistakable sparkle in her vivid green eyes. She brings light into every room and every space she inhabits, and I can feel her energy radiating outward with incredible power and with overwhelming *goodness*.

And for the first time, I *see* an aura, rather than just feeling it, and it brings tears to my eyes. Mira's aura is so vividly brilliant, shining out from her in every direction with such radiance it lights up my heart. She's bright and beautiful and glowing from within.

The same way Alexander always glowed—incandescent and breathtaking, and exuding that incredible feeling of love … and peace.

And I know in my heart that I can let go, because Alexander was right.

Our baby Miracle is going to change the world.

Epilogue

Seven years later (Sydney, Australia)

The little girl removes her shoes and socks and squishes her feet in the sand in the large sandbox she's playing in, reveling in the feel of the smooth, warm sand between her toes. She looks up, hand held over her vivid sea-blue eyes as a shield from the sun, squinting at the lone, billowy white cloud in the otherwise clear sky. She glances over at her parents, sitting on a bench nearby talking with some other parents, and then she smooths a lock of hair from her face, deposits it behind her ear, and goes back to trying to build her sandcastle with a bridge she can place her favorite figurines under.

A little boy with tousled dark hair walks over, curious. "What are you building?" he asks.

The little girl looks up, and when her cheerful blue eyes meet the boy's kind green eyes, they both stop and stare for a moment—neither sure why—and then they exchange soft smiles.

"Who are you?" the little girl asks.

"Just moved here," he answers.

"I'm Dany," she says.

"Xander," he answers.

She nods and gestures to the broken area of her castle. "I'm trying to build an arch, but it keeps crumbling on the people." She holds up the two plastic figures in her hand, caked with sand. They look like a well-worn bride and groom rescued from the top of someone's wedding cake.

Xander bends down to take a closer look, inspecting the sandcastle. He makes a notch on either side of where the arch will connect. Then he dips his hands into her plastic pail of water and uses his wet fingers to make the notches a little deeper. He turns to look at Dany, who's watching him curiously.

She smiles at him and he smiles back and they hold each other's gaze for longer than one might expect, as they sit in the warm sand under the bright blue sky.

"What are you doing?" she asks when he pours half of her water out and starts forming a big pile of wet sand.

"Fixing it," he says.

She shakes her head. "I already tried that. I don't think it will work."

He looks over at her and meets her eyes and something about his gaze feels familiar. She trusts him. "We can do this together," he says. "Watch me." He puts his hand in the space where the arch will be and starts piling heaps of wet sand onto it with the other hand and connecting the wet sand to the notches. "After it dries a little, it should stay."

She smiles and shrugs and places her hand next to his and starts piling more wet sand onto both of their hands, forming the foundation of the arch.

"What if it crashes again when we pull our hands out?" Dany asks.

"Don't worry," he says, his green eyes crinkling, making her smile. "It'll work this time. I have a plan."

True Love Stories

Never End

Thank You

Dear Reader,

I truly hope you enjoyed Declan and Alexander's story. Thank you for reading, and thank you in advance for supporting authors and helping other readers by considering leaving an online review on Amazon, Goodreads, and/or your favorite blog/website forum for romance readers. Reviews are golden to indie authors and they are so appreciated. I read them all and I thank you for taking the time.

If you enjoyed *The Guardian Series*, look for more titles coming soon. You can connect with me online at **ajmessenger.com**, **facebook.com/ajmessengerauthor**, and **@aj_messenger** on Twitter. I love hearing from you! Thanks for your kind support.

A.J. Messenger

Contact Me

Learn more about new releases and contact me

I welcome you to visit me at the sites below and subscribe to my newsletter to be the first to know about upcoming releases.

ajmessenger.com

facebook.com/ajmessengerauthor

@aj_messenger

Books by A.J. Messenger

The Guardian Series

(a paranormal angel romance series)

Guardian

(book one)

Fallen

(book two)

Revelation

(book three)

55826605R00126

Made in the USA
Middletown, DE
18 July 2019